"I want to thank you for being here for me. I don't know what I would have done today after the bombing."

But he knew, because she'd shown him her true colors today and not just during the hostage situation.

She'd shown him later with his dad and now, when she'd finally made his apartment feel like a home.

When he'd shared his work with her, something he'd never done before with anyone.

"But *I* know. You'd have been strong the way you were today. The way you were when you and your mom built new lives for yourselves. You're a strong woman. A caring woman," he said and covered her hand with his.

"Promise me one thing," she said. "Promise me you'll stay safe. *¡Cuídate!*"

Somehow the promise took on new meaning with her. Dangerous meaning because he could already imagine hearing that from her every morning. Could imagine coming home to Maisy.

And that was possibly more dangerous than the bomber, who was on the loose.

Thank you to all my friends at Liberty States Fiction Writers for offering your support and insights. A special thanks to Gwen Jones, Linda Parisi and Lois Winston for their hard work to keep Liberty States moving forward. Finally, lots of love to my daughter, Samantha, who is always there for me and is an amazing writer and photojournalist. *Saranghaeyo*, Samantha.

TRAPPING A TERRORIST

———

New York Times Bestselling Author
CARIDAD PIÑEIRO

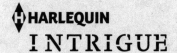

Special thanks and acknowledgment are given to Caridad Piñeiro
for her contribution to the Behavioral Analysis Unit miniseries.

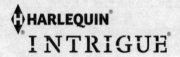

Recycling programs
for this product may
not exist in your area.

ISBN-13: 978-1-335-48913-5

Trapping a Terrorist

Copyright © 2021 by Harlequin Books S.A.

This edition published by arrangement with Harlequin Books S.A.

For questions and comments about the quality of this book,
please contact us at CustomerService@Harlequin.com.

Harlequin Enterprises ULC
22 Adelaide St. West, 40th Floor
Toronto, Ontario M5H 4E3, Canada
www.Harlequin.com

Printed in U.S.A.

New York Times and *USA TODAY* bestselling author **Caridad Piñeiro** is a Jersey girl who just wants to write and is the author of nearly fifty novels and novellas. She loves romance novels, superheroes, TV and cooking. For more information on Caridad and her dark, sexy romantic suspense and paranormal romances, please visit www.caridad.com.

Books by Caridad Piñeiro

Harlequin Intrigue

Cold Case Reopened
Trapping a Terrorist

Visit the Author Profile page at Harlequin.com.

CAST OF CHARACTERS

Miguel Peters—Miguel is an anti-terrorism expert with the FBI who is following in his mother's footsteps; she was a legend in the business but died in the line of duty. Determined to protect those he serves, Miguel doesn't see himself as having a wife and family.

Maisy Oliver—Maisy dreams of seeing the country, the world and writing about her travels. Those dreams were once shattered by her father's bombing spree in Washington State. She's finally pursuing those dreams, but will her growing feelings for Miguel change her plans?

Robert Peters—A retired journalism professor, Robert is determined to convince his son that it's time Miguel find a safer job so he can lead a normal life with a woman like Maisy.

Chris Adams—A down-and-out young man who has gotten caught up in a bombing plan intended to create fear in Seattle.

Richard Rothwell—A blowhard political candidate for state senate.

Olivia Branson—Smart and savvy, Olivia is the FBI director overseeing Miguel and his Behavioral Analysis Unit team.

Liam McDare—A genius at the keyboard, he's not as smart in love, but the current investigation will show him what really matters in life.

Prologue

I need the perfect hostage.

Tucked behind the protection of the column, he watched the people coming and going in King Street Station, unaware of the danger. Unaware that he intended to grab one of them, and soon.

Peering around the edge of the column, he spied a young boy at a nearby kiosk. The boy, who was maybe six or seven, was focused on the shelves of candy before him, eyes wide in anticipation of a treat. His distracted parents, tourists if he had to guess from the expensive camera dangling around the man's neck and the map tucked into his back pocket, were a few feet away, their attention on a display of postcards, probably to commemorate their visit to Seattle.

He laughed, thinking about how it would be a visit they would never forget if he grabbed their boy. But parents could be overly protective when their kids were involved. If the two of them went crazy when he snatched the boy, it could all go south.

Still, if this was a video game, kids would score high

points for being fast, hard to control and too young to die.

A few yards away a dainty young thing stood chatting to an older man. She was pretty in that girl-next-door kind of way. Brown hair with caramel highlights was tucked up in a feminine braid and as she glanced his way, he noticed her eyes. Blue, but a blue so deep they were almost indigo. A man could get lost in those eyes. Angel Eyes.

He imagined grabbing her, but her body was toned and no matter how angelic she looked, something about her warned that she'd be scrappy.

Again, high points for that feistiness and beauty.

Not so many points for the old man with her.

He looked like an absent-minded professor with his tweed cap, sweater with leather patches on the elbows and silver-rimmed eyeglasses that made his eyes look way too big. The professor didn't seem feeble, but he didn't seem like a problem either.

I could take him, he thought until a tall, muscular man turned to speak to Angel Eyes and the professor. The man was fit and powerful looking but leaning heavily on a cane. He looked like a younger version of the professor. Enough to maybe be a son. This man could be major trouble, but trouble would definitely earn more points in any game.

A second later the man's phone rang. He held up a finger, turned and took a few steps away, probably for privacy during the call.

Perfect. This is my chance.

Chapter One

It was a small step for most people, but a giant leap for Maisy Oliver as she hopped on the Seattle tour bus.

In the year since Maisy had made her mother a promise on her deathbed, she'd been scrimping and saving, planning on how she would leave the nastiness of her past and reach for her dreams of traveling and writing a blog about those travels. Maybe even a book one day.

Granted Seattle wasn't Paris or London or Rome, but her hometown was beautiful and as good a place as any to start on that dream.

And that dream had begun with a great new job that had allowed her to buy what she needed to start her blog and save money for the future.

Armed with a brand-new phone with the supposedly best camera ever and a small journal to take notes, she intended to share the many sights in Seattle on the blog she'd set up earlier in the week. Hopefully she'd be able to grow a following and expand her travels. A ferry across Puget Sound. The Woodinville Wine Country. Victoria in British Columbia.

Who knows where I can go from there! Even Paris, she thought as she took a seat on the top level of the bus, bouncing her feet anxiously as the bus headed for the next stop on the tour: Pike Place Market. She intended to do the whole loop on the hop-on-hop-off bus before returning to each stop to take photos and notes. She hoped that the tour would give her enough information to line up blog posts for a few weeks while she planned her next adventure.

The bus lumbered to a stop at Pike Place Market, and Maisy snapped off a few photos of the large neon Public Market and Farmers Market signs and the clock above the entrance to the various shops and stalls. As she did so she took note of the people waiting to board the bus, especially the handsome man bracing himself on a cane next to an older gentleman who had to be his father. The two looked too much alike not to be related. In front of them were a man and woman with a young boy, probably tourists if she had to guess.

But then again, she was a tourist today in her hometown.

The people boarded the crowded tour bus and the noisy clamber of someone rushing up the steps drew her attention. The young boy with the family. Barely seconds later, the older man and his son came up the stairs, the younger man wincing with each step he took.

The man was fit, in excellent shape actually, and she wondered if it was some kind of sports injury as they followed the family up the aisle and took the two seats directly opposite her. The young man was on the outside seat, his father on the aisle beside her.

The older man smiled at her and she returned it since he seemed like a nice enough person. His son… too stoic and serious. Tense, especially as his father bumped his arm and jerked his head in her direction.

The man shot her a quick look and rolled his eyes before mumbling something to his father.

Really? she thought, her ego a little stung by what seemed like a rebuff. But not stung enough to avoid the older man when he pleasantly said, "Are you enjoying the tour, young lady?"

"I am, thank you," she said.

"Are you a tourist? I'm a tourist, but my son lives in Seattle," he asked, eyes wide behind the thick lenses of his glasses.

"You might say that," she said as his son murmured, "Dad, please."

EMBARRASSED HEAT FLOODED FBI Agent Miguel Peters's cheeks as his father tried his very obvious matchmaking with the pretty woman sitting across from them on the tour bus.

He'd told his father time and time again that he had no interest in a relationship right now. Or maybe even ever. As the supervisory special agent of the Seattle Behavioral Analysis Unit, his personal time was limited. He'd thought his father would be aware of what that took, considering Miguel's mother had been a renowned BAU profiler. One who'd paid for it with her life, cementing his decision to follow in her footsteps.

But as his father kept up the conversation with the young woman, he had to admit that his father couldn't have chosen better. Not only was the young woman beautiful, with amazing blue eyes and enticing girl-next-door looks, but she seemed bright and interested. Caring as she patiently answered his father's questions and engaged him with some of her own.

"Are you enjoying your visit, Robert?" she said, and her glance skittered between his father and him.

His father likewise shot a look at him before he said, "I only just arrived a day ago, but I'm enjoying your hometown so far, Maisy."

Hometown? Miguel thought. *Great. More reason to encourage his father to continue with his matchmaking with Maisy. Maisy? What kind of name was that anyway?*

"It is lovely. That's why I decided to share it with people on my blog," the young woman said as the bus lumbered to their next stop at the Chittenden Locks. While some of the tourists on the bus hurried off, Maisy stayed back with the pair.

"Don't feel you have to stay with us," his father said.

She smiled—*She is even prettier when she smiles*, Miguel thought—and waved off Robert's suggestion.

"I'm going to stay on until the last stop at King

Street Station and take some photos there before hopping back on for the other stops," Maisy said.

As Maisy stood to snap some photos, his father elbowed him again and murmured, "Perfect."

Like Maisy, his father and he had planned on staying on the tour bus until the station and then heading to the Chihuly Garden and Glass exhibition near the Space Needle.

Determined to avoid his father's meddling and the attractive Maisy, he turned his attention to the locks, which connected the salt water of Puget Sound with the fresh water of Salmon Bay. Boats were lined up to pass through the locks, which also provided safe passage for salmon to spawn.

Barely minutes later, the bus was in motion again and in just over fifteen minutes they were pulling up in front of King Street Station. Slower than usual because of his injury, Miguel hung back, allowing the family who had come on with Maisy at Pike Place Market to rush off. Maisy and his father went next, heading down the stairs with him following, the stitches in his leg pulling with each step. But he was determined to show his father that he was fine during this visit. Especially since his father had rushed out to Seattle when he'd heard Miguel had been shot.

As Maisy and Robert left the bus and strolled toward King Street Station, they started chatting again, Miguel tagging along behind them. When they reached the station, Maisy walked toward one side, probably to take photos for the blog she had mentioned, and his father trailed afterward, leaving Miguel no choice but to go with them unless he wanted to seem antisocial. Truth be told, Maisy probably already thought that, although if she had half a brain, she'd have seen through his father's obvious attempts to get them together.

When Maisy looked in his direction, he forced himself to smile and bear it. As he did so, he noticed one of his BAU members, Lorelai Parker, the assistant to the FBI's director, waiting by the chairs at one side of the station. He was about to go say hello when his phone rang.

His BAU director was calling. Olivia Branson was in Washington, trying to secure additional funding for their office, and probably needed some information from him.

He held up a finger, turned and took a few steps away, certain that he would need privacy during the call, and he wasn't wrong.

"Good morning, Olivia."

"I wish it were. Do you have time to talk?"

Miguel glanced back toward his father and seeing that he was busy chatting with the young woman, he took the call.

Chapter Two

Perfect. This is my chance.

He reached into his pocket, pulled out a black ski mask and yanked it over his face as he hurried around the column. As he moved, he dug into his knapsack and took out a collar bomb and detonator.

The professor looked at him when he approached, eyes blinking like an owl's, but he didn't move, making it way too easy for him to slip the metal collar over the man's head and snap it tightly into place. He wrapped the arm holding the detonator around the man's chest and held up his other hand to display his cell phone, his finger resting over the speed dial number to set off another bomb in the building.

"Miguel," the professor screamed. The old man's body trembled beneath his arm, and his knees seemed to give for a second before he straightened.

The man with the cane turned at the sound of his name. His face paled and fear slipped over his features before he schooled them.

Fear was good. It was just what he needed so they'd do as he asked.

"Don't anyone move or I'll blow his head off! Or blow the second bomb!"

MIGUEL'S BLOOD RAN cold at the sight of his father with the collar bomb around his neck and the wild eyes of the masked man holding the detonator and a cell phone.

He had to stay calm even as pandemonium erupted all around. People had realized what was going on and raced away despite the bomber's threat, screaming and shoving each other to escape the danger. But as others were running from the threat, he raced toward it to save his father and the young woman nearby who hadn't moved an inch.

"You don't want to see him die now, do you?" the bomber screamed out again and waved the cell phone in the air.

Those who remained, a much smaller crowd, froze in place or took shelter behind the banks of chairs scattered around the station. Most would be safe if the collar bomb went off, but who knew where the second bomb was located?

Not to mention that Maisy was just a few feet away from his father and the bomber. Definitely in harm's way if the collar bomb exploded.

And then there was his dad, who was looking at him with wide eyes. Pleading eyes. His face was pale, as white as new snow, ramping up Miguel's fear because his dad's heart was not strong.

Miguel raised his hands, and in a calm and practiced voice, he said, "You don't want to do this. You don't want to hurt anybody."

He inched forward, slowly, deliberately, intent on trying to move Maisy out of harm's way while gauging whether he could rush the bomber and take away the detonator. If he'd been one hundred percent healthy Miguel might have been able to do it, but he wasn't one hundred percent thanks to the bullet he'd taken during an earlier investigation. Plus, he wasn't sure if the detonator had a dead switch. He needed to get closer to see, but as he did so several police officers rushed in, guns drawn.

"Stop or I'll blow you all up. I'll do it, so don't push me," the bomber said and again waved the cell phone in a wild arc above his head.

With that motion and his closer physical distance to the terrorist, the skunky smell of weed wafted over to Miguel, increasing his fear because he was now also possibly dealing with someone who was high and not thinking rationally.

The bomber pointed at him with the cell phone. "You, Mr. Hero. The professor's son, right? Step back and take those pigs with you."

Miguel slowly reached for Maisy, but the bomber called out, "No, not her. I like her. She's really pretty. Makes me calm. You want me calm, right, Angel Eyes?"

Maisy nodded, held out a hand, palm up in pleading, and in a soft voice said, "Right. You need to stay calm. I know you don't want to hurt anybody."

The bomber laughed, a laugh that bordered on unhinged, and Miguel did as he asked. He slowly backed away until he was close to one of the police officers who had raced into the station. In low tones, he said, "I'm FBI. Supervisory Special Agent Miguel Peters."

The officer nodded to confirm he'd heard, and in a whisper, asked, "What do you want us to do?"

"Nothing right now. I'm sure my team will be arriving shortly," Miguel said, trying to process as much as he could about what was happening because something was off. The more typical MO for collar bombs involved a demand for money, whether it was blackmail, a kidnapping or a bank robbery. So far, the bomber hadn't asked for a thing.

"Talk to us, man. What do you want?" he called out, trying to glean as much as he could not only from the man's actions, but from his speech. Was he a local? Level of education? Tattoos or other distinguishing features? Anything that could help in the situation or after…

He tried not to think about the after because that might mean his father was dead. Maybe the young woman as well as any of the people still trapped in the station, depending on where the second bomb was situated. He had to get those people out as soon as he could.

"What do you want?" he repeated because up until now the man hadn't said much.

"What do I want? Where do I start?" He gestured

to the officers standing nearby, guns still drawn. "I want them out. All of them or I'll blow the place and kill everyone here."

The officer closest to Miguel peered in his direction, waiting for his instructions.

"How about you let the cops take all those people out of here so we can talk?" Miguel said, and motioned to the people huddled behind plastic chairs for protection.

"And why would I want to talk to you, Mr. Hero?" the bomber said.

Miguel pointed in the direction of his father and the young woman he'd only just met. "I'm FBI and you've got my dad and girlfriend right there. We're worth lots more to you as hostages than a bunch of scared tourists and some beat cops."

The man narrowed unhinged eyes, obviously considering what Miguel had said. Then his gaze bounced around the station, almost as if doing a body count to determine if Miguel, his father and the young woman were a good trade for the people and cops in the station.

But as the bomber did so, the sound of a television intruded from a nearby kiosk, drawing the bomber's attention.

THE BOMBER'S GAZE turned toward the television and Maisy thought, *This is my chance.*

But if she moved, the man might do as he said and blow the bombs in the station and she didn't want to be responsible for that. Too many people might be hurt, including the gentle professor she'd met on the tour bus earlier that morning.

They'd been chatting up a storm on the bus and after, as they'd arrived in the station. He'd been so kind, so friendly. Probably because he'd been trying to matchmake for his stoic son, who might be handsome if he ever smiled.

She couldn't leave the old man. She wouldn't be responsible for any more murder and mayhem like her father had done. Her father, a monster who even now controlled her life.

She had to focus and find a way to get out of this. Get the professor away from the madman.

Focus, she told herself as the bomber's attention was fixated on the television.

THE SITUATION HAD already hit the airwaves and various reporters and news crews had gathered around King Street Station, broadcasting coverage.

Behind the on-scene reporter advising on the hostage situation, Miguel noticed Lorelai standing nearby. He hoped that she had alerted his team to what was happening so that they would be on their way to the station.

"Good afternoon, this is Drew Anderson reporting for Seattle One News. We're here at King Street Station, where a bomber has taken an older man hostage with the use of what authorities are calling a collar bomb. The suspect also claims to have a second bomb that he will detonate if his demands are not met, but no demands have been forthcoming so far. Authorities estimate that there are still about two hundred people trapped in the station. At this time, all trains coming and going from the station have been locked down while authorities deal with the situation."

The reporter paused and looked off camera and a second later another familiar face came on air.

"We have with us Caitlyn Yang, the Seattle Behavioral Analysis Unit's police liaison. Can you give us a report on what the FBI is doing about this hostage crisis, Caitlyn?"

"Thank you, Drew," she said with a nod to the reporter before facing the camera. "At the request of the local police, the FBI team is coordinating with them on the case. One of our agents is inside with the bomber—"

Before she could finish, Richard Rothwell, a candidate for state senator, pushed his way into camera range. As the reporter turned his attention to him, Rothwell looked directly into the camera and said, "We don't negotiate with terrorists—we outsmart them. I have a plan on my website and never fear, Seattle, I'm here for you because I'm not afraid of the sociopath inside our beloved King Street Station. But please stay home for your safety because I care about *you*." He emphasized the latter by imitating Uncle Sam pointing into the camera.

Miguel gritted his teeth and tried his best not to

roll his eyes at the candidate's grandstanding, which would do nothing to help the situation. It might even make things worse with the unstable unsub.

"Listen to him, will ya? Sociopath," the bomber said with a wild laugh. "The Feds, boys in blue and some pompous politician won't stop me." He waved the cell phone around in the air again and said, "If I don't get what I want, I'll blow this place."

"Why don't you tell me what you want," Miguel said.

"What I want? Let's start off by taking down our inept government and judicial systems. How about prison reform? No bail requirements. Free housing and medical insurance for all."

Miguel couldn't really consider them demands because there was little anyone could do to satisfy them in order to defuse the situation. But he had to try.

"I get it, man. Government isn't really there to help us, right? But I'll try to help you. Just tell me one thing you want right now."

For a second the bomber lowered the hand with the cell phone and in a steadier voice he said, "I want a ham sandwich."

"I can do that," Miguel said, but a breath later a powerful explosion took out the balcony above them, raining down bits of concrete, marble and other debris. He was knocked off his feet with the force of the blast.

Stunned, ears ringing, Miguel sluggishly got to

his knees. His father, the bomber and the young woman were all lying flat on the floor.

Fear knotted his gut. *Did the collar bomb go off as well?* he thought and tried to process whether there had been more than one explosion. Whether there had been a second one that he hadn't heard over the force, concussion and confusion from the first blast.

But then the bomber slowly sat up, the detonator still in his hand. He looked dazed, confused. Possibly surprised by the blast.

Did the second bomb go off accidentally? Miguel considered, but then another thought hit him.

This is my chance.

Chapter Three

Miguel shot toward the trio, but his wounded leg gave out beneath him. Frustrated, he pushed on, scrambling, almost crawling to get to the bomber. To get to the detonator before the unsub blew the collar bomb.

To his surprise, the bomber dropped the detonator, struggled to his feet and rushed away.

Miguel went to give chase, but his wounded leg tripped him up again and he knew it was useless. He grabbed his cell phone and called Madeline Striker, the most senior of his agents. She answered, but his ears were still ringing so badly he could barely hear her, and his father was starting to move, propelling fear through his gut again.

"Don't move, Dad. Don't move," he shouted as his father rose to a sitting position and fear ripped through him. *I can't lose him. Not like this. Not like Mami*, he thought, angry with himself that he couldn't do more.

"Miguel. Are you okay?" Madeline said, her voice garbled and indistinct beneath the ringing in his ears.

"Unsub is heading out of the northwest corner of the building. About five foot eight. White. Brown eyes. Wearing blue jeans, black T-shirt, stained gray sweatshirt, black leather gloves and a black ski mask. Copy?" he asked, and at her affirmative reply, he rushed to kneel beside his father.

"Are you okay, Dad?" he asked, but even as he did that, he kept his head and used his jacket sleeve to secure the detonator without touching it to preserve any fingerprints.

Maisy slipped to their side, but he held his hand up to stop her. "Don't come any closer. Not until we can defuse the bomb."

She nodded and knelt there, smudges of dirt on her face. Bits of debris in her hair and on her clothing. There was an angry abrasion above one eye where she might have been struck by shrapnel from the blast. "Are you okay?" she asked his dad, concern ringing in her tone.

His father nodded and Miguel again admonished, "Please don't move, Dad. We've got to get this off you."

"Please stay still, Robert. It will be okay," Maisy said and took hold of his father's hand.

Miguel crouched beside her and laid a hand on her shoulder. It felt fragile beneath his hand, but he sensed there was steel in her core as she said, "I'm not leaving him, whoever you are."

"FBI. Supervisory Special Agent Miguel Peters," he replied.

She looked at him with those amazing blue eyes the bomber had fixated on and with a nod, she said, "You'd best get to work, then."

He knew she wouldn't relent and leave his father's side.

"Are you feeling all right, Dad?" he said, worried about his father's heart condition.

"I am," his father said without moving a muscle. "Don't worry about me and do your job. It's what your mother would have done."

Even with the gamut of emotions roiling through him, Miguel knew his father was right and didn't waste any more time arguing with them.

He rose and peered around the station, taking in the destruction. A large chunk of the balcony several yards from them had been blown away and pieces of it were scattered all about the main floor of the station. The force of the blast had overturned chairs in the area and shattered nearby windows. Luckily, the explosion hadn't ignited a fire.

The people who had been trapped in the station had rushed out when they realized the bomber had fled, and there was now an eerie silence inside the space, interrupted only by the continued ringing in his ears.

There were a great deal of police and his team had to get to work, Miguel thought as he limped to get his cane, picked it up and then slowly moved toward the door, the wound in his leg sending shards of pain through him with each step.

Almost as if they'd heard him, his team members walked in together with an officer from the Seattle Arson Bomb Squad. They waited for him by the entrance to the station, not wanting to contaminate the scene.

He walked over, careful not to disturb any evidence. When he reached them, he slipped into his role as the SSA, pushing back his personal fear for his father. His frustration at not being one hundred percent, which had let the bomber escape. He looked at Madeline and said, "The unsub?"

Madeline shook her head. "No sign of him, Miguel. But the news crews were filming all around the area and we're hoping they might have caught something. We've also asked SPD to get the names of everyone who just left the station so we can interview them."

"Good work, Madeline," he said.

The Seattle ABS officer, Mack Gonzalez, was a friend he'd worked with before. The officer said, "We need to keep the area clear until I defuse that collar bomb. Don't worry, Miguel. I'll take care of your dad."

"Is the perimeter secure? Have you checked for any other secondary devices? Car bombs to take out the first responders?"

"Perimeter is secure and we're checking all vehicles in the area. HAZMAT team detectors haven't picked up anything toxic. Same with radiation detection, so for now, we're good," Mack confirmed.

"Got it, Mack. We'll stay out of your way while you work on my dad, and thank you," Miguel said and clapped the other man on the back of the padded uniform.

He glanced at his team, knowing that they would be itching to move on this case, but there were a number of things they could work on back at the BAU offices. The local ABS and police would collect the evidence and forward them the information they needed to develop their profile and round up additional information to help the locals with their investigation.

"Lorelai, you were here earlier, correct?" he asked.

At that, Liam McDare, their tech guru, went to slip an arm around his ex-fiancée, but she scuttled away from him.

"I was waiting for a friend. I called the team as soon as I saw what was happening. Director Branson as well," she said, always the efficient administrative assistant.

"Excellent. I was on the phone with Olivia so I'm glad you've told her what's occurred. Now I need all of you to get going. Nicholas and Madeline, start interviewing those in the station and get to work on a profile. FYI, no real demands were made before the explosion. Except for a ham sandwich."

"A ham sandwich?" Nicholas asked. As his top serial killer profiler, Miguel relied on Nicholas's expertise in that area and others.

"That's the only real request. The rest weren't realistic demands," Miguel said with a nod and turned his attention to Madeline, who had both personal and professional experience with kidnappers. "Collar bombs like this one are often used in kidnapping or blackmail scenarios. Run those ideas up the flagpole with Nicholas."

He looked at the other agents gathered there. "Liam and Dash. Please round up any video feeds you can from the reporters, CCTV, ATMs, surveillance cameras. Get any images available and run them through facial recognition. Do background checks. You can get David to help you as needed. You know the drill."

"Got it, boss," Dash said with a dip of his head and his team sprang into action, rushing out the door to handle the tasks Miguel had assigned.

Miguel returned his attention to where the ABS officer was kneeling beside his father and the young woman. The officer was in the large, padded suit worn by bomb squad specialists, making him appear gargantuan compared to his father and the woman.

As carefully as he had walked over, Miguel returned, cautiously picking his way past any possible evidence. He scanned the area for any details that might clue them in to the identity of the bomber and his MO. He picked out small bits of paper that looked like dynamite stick wrappers, as well as pieces of black leather and blue wire, but that didn't make sense. The dynamite and leather pointed toward a briefcase bomb, which was at odds with the box secured around his father's neck. That looked like it contained pipe bombs.

Two different MOs? he thought as he neared the trio.

"You really should leave," Mack said to the young woman as he worked on the collar of the bomb.

"I'm not going to leave Robert alone," Maisy said and vehemently shook her head.

"He's not alone. Mack and I are here," Miguel said, his heart pounding in his chest as the ABS officer fiddled with the hinged collar around his father's neck, trying to unlock the device. The officer muttered something under his breath, but a second later he snapped the collar open and eased the bomb away.

"Something wrong?" Miguel asked, hands jammed on his hips as he watched the officer slowly rise with the bomb and take a few steps back.

Mack shook his head. "I don't think this detonator is connected, but I need to take this somewhere safer to finish defusing it."

Miguel nodded. "You'll give me your full report when you have it?"

"You got it, Miguel," Mack said and walked off, cradling the device as delicately as if it was fragile crystal.

Relief slammed through Miguel that his father was safe, and he stepped closer to him and the young woman. "Let's get you both outside and have the EMTs check you out." He lent his father a hand so he could stand and so did Maisy. Together they helped him to his feet.

As she rose, she looked down and said, "You're bleeding."

Miguel risked a quick glance at his leg where blood had leaked through his khaki pants, probably because he'd torn open the stitches in his leg. "I'm okay. Let's get out of here," he said, and it occurred to him then that he didn't really know who she was.

He held out his hand. "And you are Maisy…?"

She shook his hand. "Oliver. Maisy Oliver," she said, providing him the last name he'd wanted.

Outside, the EMTs quickly got to work, checking all of them for signs of injuries from the blast as well as his dad's heart and Miguel's leg. Luckily, he'd only torn open a couple of stitches. It was easy enough to repair the minor damage.

As the EMT worked on him, his father stood nearby, worry etched onto his features. "Your mother would have been so proud of you today. So proud of the way you handled that situation."

"Thank you, Dad," he said, but braced himself for what he was sure would follow.

"But you risked your life today. Again. It's why I'd hoped you'd choose a safer kind of work. I don't want to lose you too."

Miguel bit his lip and looked away, fighting back an angry retort. His father only wanted the best for him, and he understood his pain. He'd lost the love of his life to the FBI and a terrorist's bullet. But nothing his father said would change his mind about his choice of career. He did it for his mother and for people like Maisy and his father, who didn't deserve to be in harm's way.

"I understand what you want, Dad. But this is my job."

He turned to Maisy and said, "Thank you so much for staying with my father. That was very brave."

"I had to do it," she said and smiled at his father.

He nodded and pressed on. "You're a witness, Dad. I'm going to have to get you settled in a safe house until we catch the bomber. Same with you, Maisy, especially since he's fixated on you for some reason," he said.

Maybe because she's gorgeous, he thought. With the danger over he could fully appreciate the woman standing before him. A beautiful woman with a spine of steel, tons of courage and a truly caring heart based on what he'd seen of her so far.

MAISY KNEW WHAT it was like to be the object of an unhinged person's obsession.

Her father had terrorized Washington State with a series of explosions at various logging and construction sites. During her father's reign of terror, he'd maimed and injured many people and killed one at the site of his last bombing.

He'd been in prison for the last fifteen years and she'd been free of him for most of that time, but then a year ago he'd found her and started a second reign of terror with weekly letters and collect phone calls from the prison. She'd sent the letters back unopened and refused the calls, but that hadn't stopped him.

Much like she worried that the FBI agent was right that the bomber wouldn't stop with her either.

But she refused to let her life be controlled by another terrorist the way her father had dominated her.

"I had to stay with your father, but I'm not going to a safe house," she said and tilted her chin up at a determined angle.

"My dear, it's what makes sense," Robert said and laid a gentle hand on her arm.

"I'm not going, Robert," she reiterated, but his son was having none of it.

"You *are* going. If not into a safe house, we'll provide you with a protective detail," Miguel said.

"And who's going to make me do it? You? Will you protect me?" she challenged, hating how childish it sounded, but determined to be the master of her own fate. It had been her primary goal since her mother's death to finally follow her dreams.

Miguel tapped his chest. "Yes, me, if I have to. You're a material witness and I need to keep you safe," he said, his brown eyes almost black with worry. Bits of dust clung to the thick waves of his dark hair and she unconsciously reached up to brush them away, but then jerked her hand back. The gesture would have been too intimate. One of lovers and not the strangers they were.

"You?" she repeated and blew out a harsh breath. "You'd really agree to be my protective detail?"

With a huff, he jammed his hands on his hips and firmed his jaw. "You got a problem with that?"

She had lots of problems with it, especially now that she had the time to realize what a devastatingly handsome man he was and how hard it would be to ignore that and the gentle and caring way he'd dealt with his father. But a bomber was on the loose and fixated on her, and they were lucky that no one had been hurt today.

They might not be so lucky again if Miguel didn't do his job. And because she knew that they didn't have time to waste, she nodded and said, "I'll go. But only with you. And I have to call my boss and let him know what's happening."

Miguel seemed taken aback by her acquiescence but clearly wasn't going to argue. He held a finger up and said, "I need to make a call to get the safe house ready for my dad."

He limped away for a moment to phone and as he did so, Robert laid a hand on her arm. His touch was soothing, and for a too brief moment, it reminded her of her father's gentle touch before she'd discovered he was a monster. "He means well, Maisy. Don't judge him too harshly. He's just been…determined since his mother was killed."

"And you've been worried for him," she said and covered Robert's hand with her own, once again sensing the earlier tension between the two men.

Robert nodded and his silver-rimmed glasses slipped on his nose before he pushed them up with his index finger. "I have. It was so hard to lose my wife. I don't want to lose him as well. He's all I have left."

She didn't have time to respond since at that moment Miguel returned to their side. "The safe house will be ready shortly. We should go get your things from the hotel, Dad. Same for you, Maisy. We can run by your place so you can pack a bag."

She tipped her chin up, trying to stay strong even though fear was starting to blossom through her now that the adrenaline was wearing off. But she couldn't let the fear take over. After all, that was the purpose of terrorism, wasn't it? To create fear.

"I'm ready," she said, but for what, she didn't rightly know.

Chapter Four

Dashiell West watched over Liam as the man worked on cleaning up the images they had been able to get from the CCTV cameras in King Street Station. In addition to sharpening the images, which were not the best quality, Liam had to address the position of the bomber's body. Once Liam had done that, adjusting the lean, tilt and orientation of the photo, he'd use another program to adjust those variables in order to create an image which could be run against their various databases.

Dashiell walked over to another desk, where David Dyson, their twenty-something intern, was combing through various video feeds and surveillance cameras in the area, trying to locate other images of the bomber which would not only help identify him, but maybe also pinpoint the direction he might have gone after the explosion. "How's it going?" Dash asked.

David looked up at him and smiled, his brown eyes gleaming with intelligence and determination. David had lost a beloved uncle during a convenience store robbery and that had prompted the young man to begin a career in law enforcement instead of going into the private sector with his skills.

"Doing great. I've got one video so far and am using the location of that camera to look for others in the area," David said.

Dash clapped the young man on the shoulder. "Good job. Keep it up."

"You know I will," David said, his grin broadening with Dash's praise.

Dashiell walked away to his own desk, but as he did so, he noticed Lorelai Parker walk in. Liam's head immediately turned in the direction of his ex-fiancée. When Lorelai had called earlier to advise about the situation, Liam had almost been beside himself with worry that she was in danger. It only confirmed to Dashiell that there were still strong feelings there on both sides despite their canceled nuptials. He also suspected that Lorelai wouldn't still be so angry if she didn't care for Liam.

But their little wedding drama had to take a back seat to finding the bomber, he thought as he walked over to where Lorelai was handing an envelope to Madeline and Nicholas.

His fellow agents had been busy setting up their board at one end of the office space, placing a grainy photo of the bomber at the top of the board along with some preliminary information.

Like the fact that there had been no real demands

at King Street Station and nothing else so far, including a claim of responsibility for the bombing.

He didn't need to be a profiling expert like Madeline or Nicholas to know that made no sense.

He approached them, wondering what was in the envelope.

"Seattle ABS sent it over. Agent Gonzalez asked that you give him a call," Lorelai explained and then quickly left the room, but not before shooting a quick glance to where Liam was working.

"What have we got?" Dashiell asked and peered at the photos that Nicholas removed from the envelope and spread out on the surface of the worktable.

"Whoa, bomb collar. Looks like the one from the Pizza Bomber case," Dash said, recalling the incident where a pizza delivery man had been murdered during a bizarre bank robbery several years earlier.

"It does. The second bomb appears to have been concealed in a briefcase," Madeline said and gestured to the photos of the bits and pieces that the local police had gathered at the scene, including a fairly large piece of a briefcase handle.

"Let's get Mack on the line and see what else he's got to say." Dash dialed the ABS officer using the speakerphone and the man answered on the first ring.

"ABS Officer Gonzalez," he said.

Madeline, being the most senior agent between them, took charge. "Special Agent Striker here, Mack. We got your package. What can you tell us?"

"Madeline. Thanks for any assist BAU can give us

on this. The bomb around Miguel's dad's neck looks like a copycat of the Pizza Bomber, but it's different in several key elements. For starters there was no timer or secondary way to detonate the device. Also, no dead switch. Plus, the detonator wasn't actually connected to the pipe bombs inside the metal box holding them."

Dashiell, Madeline and Nicholas all shared a look.

"Is it possible that the connection came loose while the bomber was transporting it?" Madeline asked.

"Possible, but unlikely. There were fuses in the bombs, but the detonator wire was too short to reach the battery that would send the charge to the fuses. Either we were lucky he wasn't a good bomb maker or he didn't intend to blow the device."

"But they were real pipe bombs?" Nicholas pressed.

"Definitely. Filled with gunpowder, BBs and nails. If they had gone off, they would have likely killed whoever was wearing it and the shrapnel would have injured anyone within yards of the bomb," Mack noted and plowed on. "We were able to get partial prints off the pipes, detonator and a handle. Also, some DNA that we're already processing."

Madeline pursed her lips and nodded. "What can you tell us about the second device? It looks like a briefcase bomb."

"Confirmed. We have a big piece of the handle as well as bits and pieces of the briefcase and the wire.

Initial testing and other evidence indicate he used dynamite in the second bomb. Detonated it with a cell phone."

Nicholas shook his head. "Two different MOs in one bombing. Atypical, isn't it?"

A long sigh came across the line from the ABS officer. "It is atypical. Not to mention that dynamite is highly regulated. Luckily, it was a small blast, and the briefcase was placed in a little-used location. Only superficial damage to the structure and even better, we had only minor injuries and no fatalities."

"Almost as if he didn't want to hurt anyone," Madeline suggested.

"It seems that way. We're sending both devices to the Terrorist Explosive Device Analytical Center at Quantico so they can confirm what was used and provide more information on the devices. ATF is also working on it."

"If TEDAC agrees, we'll have to track down who can supply dynamite in the area and who has access to it," Dashiell said.

"Bingo. In the meantime, we're waiting on BAU to give us a profile or anything else you can dig up to help. We'll keep you posted, as well," Mack said.

"Can you send us the info on the fingerprints and DNA samples? Pictures of the bomb pieces?" Madeline asked.

"Will do, Madeline," Mack confirmed and signed off.

Dash waited as Madeline crossed her arms and

glanced at the team, her tall, athletic body in its dark blue suit canted at an angle. She was clearly assessing the information they'd just received, a deep furrow of worry across the brown skin of her forehead. "The object of terrorism is to create terror, so why do we have a bomber who makes no real demands, besides a ham sandwich?" she said with a chuckle and shake of her head. "And who doesn't seem to want to hurt anyone."

"Or is it an amateur?" Miguel Peters said as he walked in, his gait measured, the cane gone, almost as if Miguel thought using it was a sign of weakness. He'd changed into his standard white shirt, rep tie and dark suit. "What do we have here?" the SSA asked.

Madeline filled him in on what the Seattle ABS and PD had so far.

Miguel shook his head. "From the first I got the sense there was something off about the bomber. He didn't make his demands right away and when he did, they were way out there. We haven't received any kind of communication or manifesto, right?" His keen dark gaze skipped over all the members of the team.

"Nothing so far," Nicholas said and looked toward Madeline, who was the BAU expert on kidnappings.

"Nothing, and that type of bomb is one that's been used either in blackmail, kidnappings or bank robberies, all crimes that require precise and timely demands, usually for money," Madeline clarified.

"No real demands. No real detonator. No real injuries since the force of the bomb blast was minor despite the damage it did to the building," Miguel said and began to pace, his gait slightly stilted, as he tossed out the facts they had so far.

"Anything from the videos yet?" he asked Dashiell.

"Liam has images from the station and is working on them so we can process them against various databases. David tracked down video that had views of the bomber from a nearby source. He's searching for other videos in the area so we can possibly narrow where the bomber may have gone," he said.

Miguel nodded and jammed his fists on his hips. "My father and Maisy Oliver, the other key witness to the bombing, are both being safeguarded. I've got some preliminary testimony from them, but let's work with what we've got right now."

Miguel glanced past them as Liam approached, an almost guilty look on his face. "Boss, I've got something weird here," he said.

Liam glanced at Dash, obviously unsure about what he was about to say. "What is it, Liam?" Dash pressed.

Liam nodded and directed his attention to the SSA. "It's about Maisy Oliver."

Miguel's features hardened into stone, his lips in a grim line as he glared at their tech guru.

"What do you have for us?" Miguel said, his voice calm despite his tense body posture.

"I can't find her in the system before age fourteen. Her mother's missing history as well," Liam advised nervously, his gaze darting around the faces of the team to see how they were receiving the information.

Miguel peered at Dashiell. "Can you confirm this, Dash?"

He raised his hands to slow things down. "I was working on a tweak to our facial recognition system because we've got poor images of the bomber, not to mention the ski mask he was wearing."

Miguel dipped his head in acknowledgment. The tension in his body eased, but only somewhat. "I appreciate that. But can you work to confirm what Liam has uncovered? Find out what you can about any possible gap and let me know."

"Will do, Miguel," he said with a nod.

Miguel drew in a breath, nostrils flaring, and released it in a rush. "We've got our work cut out for us. Please get back to it and in the meantime, I'm going to speak to Ms. Oliver and see what she has to say about the bomber and those missing years."

MAISY HAD BEEN pacing back and forth in Miguel's apartment, trying to do what he had asked: recollect any details about what had happened before, during and after the bombing.

She walked to the windows of the skyscraper and looked toward the waters of Elliott Bay and beyond that, Puget Sound. Along the shoreline, assorted boats and ferries moved across the water to Bainbridge Island and other nearby locations while others pushed northward to Victoria in British Columbia.

Even as she stared at the beauty below, her mind replayed all the ugliness of that day. How she'd been standing there, chatting with Miguel's charming father, a retired professor of journalism. She'd been telling him about her new travel blog when the bomber had taken him hostage.

Shutting her eyes, she tried to remember if she'd seen the bomber before that. She vaguely recollected someone moving from behind a column. Slipping something over their face while slinging a knapsack off their shoulders.

The bomber, she realized, eyes snapping wide open.

The snick of the door lock had her whirling around in fear until she remembered that an FBI Agent was stationed at her door for protection.

A second later, Miguel entered and closed the door behind him. His entrance brought immediate peace, surprising her since they'd only known each other a few hours. But in that time, she'd come to know he was caring, honorable and courageous. Add in the fact that he was lethally handsome, and it was a potent, and possibly irresistible, combination.

But as her gaze met his, her earlier fear about being in danger morphed into a different one: he knew she wasn't what she seemed.

He walked over, his dark gaze locked on hers, assessing. Raising his hand, he gestured in the direction of the sofa and said, "Please. We need to talk."

Her gut knotted tightly, dreading what would follow. Dreading the past that she and her mother had tried so hard to outrun but which had chased them for the past fifteen years. Hoping to divert the discussion, she said, "I remembered seeing the bomber before he grabbed your father. He raced around a column without his mask for a hot second."

Miguel nodded and took the seat kitty-corner to the sofa as she sat. "Do you think you could describe what you saw? The shape of his face? Other distinguishing features?"

"Maybe," she said, a little reluctantly. It had been only a fleeting glimpse.

Miguel nodded and hesitated, almost as if searching for how to begin. Calmly, patiently, he briefly explained some of what his team was doing and finished with, "We're running the images through facial recognition. We also ran your image and did a background check. We got back incomplete results. I'm hoping you can fill in some information for me."

"Like?" she asked, well aware of where he was going and yet hoping to avoid it since it could only bring her pain as well as possibly his distrust.

He quirked a brow, seeing through her ruse. Despite that, he was composed as he said, "You know what we found. Or should I say what we didn't find. Care to explain?"

MIGUEL DIDN'T WANT to treat her like a suspect, especially considering how caring and concerned she'd been with his father. How strong to remain behind and calm him as Mack had worked to free his dad from the bomb. But until he heard from her about the gap in her history, she was now a suspect. That was the reason he'd kept out important details when he'd given her the rundown of what the BAU team had been working on.

As her almost violet gaze sheened with tears, she looked away, a sure sign of unease. Her hands were in her lap and laced tightly together. The knuckles white from the pressure.

"Maisy?" he urged, needing to hear the story from her lips. *Kissable lips*, he thought and forced away that realization. Beauty sometimes hid incredible malevolence. Not to mention that a relationship or where it would lead was not in his future.

"My mother and I moved from Woodinville to Seattle about fifteen years ago. When we did so, we changed our names because we wanted to rebuild our lives." A sniffle followed her words and she swiped away a tear.

Miguel leaned closer and laid a hand on her knee, wanting to offer comfort, but also wanting to know more. "Why, Maisy? Why did you have to change your names?"

Slowly, almost as if it pained her, she faced him with shattered eyes. "My name used to be Elizabeth Green. My father was Richard Green, the Forest Conservation Bomber."

Miguel widened his eyes, surprised by the revelation. "I'm well familiar with Green. Your father. My mother worked the case, and her profile was instrumental in helping to catch him."

"I'm glad she did before he could hurt anyone else. What he did…" She drew in a long breath and the words escaped her in a rush. "He was a monster, and we didn't know it, even though people thought we should."

Miguel remembered all the publicity about the bombings and the capture. It had turned into a media circus, almost as much of a big deal as the capture of the Unabomber. The press had hounded Green's family until they'd disappeared and now, he knew why.

"It must have been very difficult for you, Maisy," he said, trying to get her to relax and tell him more about the experience and the very odd coincidence. *A bomber's daughter being almost killed by a different bomber?* Maybe too much coincidence, although his gut was saying she wasn't involved in what had happened.

Maisy nodded and gazed down at her hands. "It was. Neighbors shunned us and our friends… You find out just who your friends are. In our case there weren't many. Almost everyone thought that my mother and I should have known what he was doing, especially my mom since she worked at the landscaping business."

Remembering the case, he said, "That's where your father assembled his bombs."

Maisy did a quick bob of her head. "It was, but

my mother was in the office or at the register tending to customers. It was a successful business. She wasn't in the sheds where my father did his evil."

Miguel covered her hands with his and squeezed gently, touched by her pain. "I can't imagine how difficult it must have been for you. You were victims as much as those injured by your father's bombs. Was that when you decided to move from Woodinville?"

HIS HAND WAS warm on hers, the palm rough. He had long elegant fingers, almost those of an artist. His simple touch, one of caring, and his words of understanding, filled her with peace once more.

"It is, and since we were starting over, it only seemed right to change our names. The court was understanding and did it without much trouble. We tried our best to stay out of the public eye, working odd jobs. Barely making it. I managed to finish high school and college," she said, but his sharp investigator's gaze saw past what she was saying.

"But you've been in a prison as much as your father has, haven't you?"

She nodded and fought against the pinching of her throat to say, "He's controlled my life even though he's been behind bars for the past fifteen years. Especially in the last year since my mother passed from cancer. Somehow, he found out my new name and address. He's been writing and calling me almost every week."

Miguel applied gentle pressure to her hand again

and as his gaze settled on hers, his eyes were a cocoa brown and filled with compassion. "I'm so sorry about your mom."

"Thank you," she barely eked out, the pain still too fresh.

"Have you responded to your father?"

She shook her head vehemently and the motion made her wince since she was a little sore from the impact of the bomb blast. "No. I want nothing to do with him. Nothing. I just want to get on with my life. With the dreams he stole from me."

Dreams of adventure and writing. The travel blog she had planned on starting with the photos from the bus tour. Which suddenly made her remember. "I was taking photos right before the bomber rushed out. I can send them to you if you'd like."

"I'd appreciate that," he said and spelled out his email address for her.

After she finished sending him the photos, he said, "It's late. Almost dinner time. I'm not much of a cook as you can probably tell from my kitchen and fridge."

"Pretty empty," she said, much like the apartment in general. It was minimalist with little personality. Totally unlike the man sitting beside her, who radiated power and confidence with his very presence and made her want to learn more about him.

"I don't spend much time here. I'm usually in the BAU office. It's on the top floor of this building," he said and pointed upward.

It struck her as kind of sad. "You live where you work?"

"It's convenient," he shot back quickly, almost defensively.

She recognized the tone. She'd overheard it on the bus before his father had started talking to her and later, when the EMTs had been tending to Miguel's leg. His father had said that he wished Miguel had a safer job and she suspected that his father also wished Miguel would one day have a family. Something that wasn't going to happen to someone who lived to work.

"I didn't mean to be judgmental. You do something very important. You keep people safe," she said, appreciating the sacrifices he made as an FBI agent.

"And I promise to keep you safe and not just from this bomber. From your father as well. You can trust me on that," he said and slowly rose from the chair, grimacing slightly as he did so.

"How's the leg? Were you hurt during a case?" she asked.

"I was shot during a recent investigation and the leg's still a little weak. It's why I was using the cane for some extra support. Thanks to the explosion, the leg's sore again along with other parts of my body. You?"

"Sore," she said and rubbed the shoulder that had hit the ground hard when she'd been knocked off her feet by the blast. She was sure she already had a bruise.

"Then let's get you dinner so you can get some rest. How do you feel about pizza?"

"You can never go wrong with pizza," she said. Her mother and she had eaten it often because they enjoyed it, it was inexpensive and it provided them with leftovers for other meals.

"I'll order and go pick it up. Would you mind setting some places at the breakfast bar?"

"Not at all. I'll be waiting for you."

Chapter Five

Dinner with Maisy was turning out to be more than Miguel had expected.

She was smart. Funny. Passionate. That was obvious from the way she told him about her dreams to travel and start a blog detailing those experiences.

"Is that why you were on the bus tour?" he asked, interested in her and not just as a suspect, which worried him. He had no room in his life for entanglements.

"It is. I've been setting aside money each paycheck in the hopes of visiting other places, but I thought, why not start with Seattle? There are lots of people who haven't been here and it's a beautiful city," she said and finished her second slice of pizza.

"It is a beautiful city. I love the water and mountains all around. It's very different from where I grew up."

She smiled and tapped the tabletop, as if confirming something to herself. "I could hear a slight singsong in your accent and there's your name. Are you Latino?"

He nodded, took a bite of his slice and after he finished, he said, "I was born and raised in Miami. My mother was Cuban and taught me Spanish."

Maisy set down the third slice of pizza she had grabbed and laid her hand on his arm. "You miss her, don't you?"

Miguel nodded. "I do. She was an amazing FBI agent. Intelligent. Brave."

Maisy shook her head, making him quiet abruptly. "You miss your *mom*. The woman who held your hand when you were sick and made your favorite dish for your birthday."

His throat tightened with emotion and for a moment, he almost couldn't breathe as the memories of his mother flooded back. The little things that mothers did, much as Maisy had so astutely pointed out. Things that his mother had done despite also being a top-notch FBI agent.

Much like you could also do, the little voice in his head said.

"She was an awesome mom," he choked out and set aside his plate, his appetite gone.

"I'm sorry," Maisy said and laid down her slice. "I didn't mean to bring back sad memories."

He shook his head. "Not sad ones at all. Good ones. Sometimes you forget the good because you're all caught up with the bad."

IF ANYONE UNDERSTOOD what it was to let the good memories get lost because of the bad, it was Maisy. "I get it, but sometimes the bad… It's impossible to forget those. To forgive them."

Miguel nodded. "Your dad. Was he a good dad?"

Maisy shrugged, trying to balance the way her dad had been when she was a child against what he'd become. "When I was little, he was always there. Caring. Loving. But as I got older, he became more and more distant. Harder. No matter what my mom tried he kept on pulling away and then we found out why."

"He'd become the Forest Conservation Bomber," Miguel said, voice flat.

His tone made her wonder if he also thought her mother and she should have known or at least suspected. "We didn't know. Didn't suspect. The landscaping business had been doing really well and we both just thought he was busy because there was so much to do."

Miguel hesitated, creating worry in her again, but instead he said, "Speaking of fathers. I should go see how my dad is doing. Would you like to go?"

She nodded. "I'd like that. It would be nice to see that he's okay. Plus, he had mentioned helping me with my blog, him being into journalism and all."

With that, they finished dinner, cleaned up and headed to the safe house, a room in a nearby hotel that was only a few blocks away. With Miguel's apartment being only a studio, there hadn't been room for both Robert and Maisy. Maisy couldn't help but notice that unlike the smaller hotel where his dad had been earlier, this one was bigger and obviously more secure. There were doormen at the front entrance and a security guard patrolled the lobby. Discreet cameras were visible in the lobby, elevators and hallways. Upstairs in Robert's room, they were greeted by another FBI agent, who stepped out to give them some privacy.

Maisy hugged the older man as they entered, and he seemed pleased with their visit.

"How are you, my dear?" he asked and slowly settled into a comfy chair in the suite's living room.

"Sore, as I imagine you are," she said and sat across from him on the sofa.

"A bit. I hope my son is treating you well," Robert said and shot a look at Miguel, who stood off to one side, arms across his chest.

"He is and hopefully this will be over quickly." She didn't want her dreams dashed before they'd even really gotten started.

Robert smiled and nodded. "If anyone can solve this, it's Miguel. He's just like his mother that way."

"Thanks," Miguel said and visibly tensed.

In the short time she'd known both men, Maisy knew the subject of Miguel's mom and Robert's wife was a touchy one and so she changed the topic.

"I would love your advice about my blog," she said, and Robert latched on to that subject with passion, offering many suggestions on what she could post on the blog and how to incorporate social media to grow her following.

After a spirited discussion, Robert said, "I so miss dealing with young minds like yours, but my university had a mandatory retirement age."

Which sparked an idea in Maisy. "Why don't you

start your own blog to share that experience? It would be so helpful to people like me."

Robert colored with the praise and nodded. "That sounds like a wonderful idea. I'd be delighted if you could help me."

"I'd love that," she said with a broad smile.

"And I'd love to let you keep brainstorming, but I have to get back to the team. Maybe you and Maisy can coordinate at another time?" Miguel said.

"We can. I understand you have important work to do," Robert said, and Miguel once again tensed, waiting for the shoe to drop, only it didn't. "I will call you tomorrow to continue this discussion."

"I'd like that," she said and rattled off her phone number. Repeated it for him as he wrote it down on a nearby pad of paper.

"Tomorrow, then," Robert said and stood just as the FBI agent guarding them returned with a bag whose smells filled the room.

"Dinner," the agent said and held up the bag.

"Enjoy and thank you for watching my dad," Miguel said as they walked to the door.

"My pleasure. Anything for you, SSA Peters," the agent said and walked toward the dining area in the suite.

Robert joined them at the door, where they exchanged goodbyes, but as they were about to step outside, his father said, *"¡Cuídate!"*

"I will," Miguel said, his voice choked, prompting Maisy to wonder.

Out in the hallway, Miguel turned to her and said, "It means 'Take care.' He used to say it to my mother whenever she left on an assignment."

So much pain, she thought as they walked back to the blue-glass skyscraper overlooking Puget Sound that housed Miguel's home and the BAU offices.

No, not his home, his prison, she thought. He was as much a prisoner of his past as she was, but at least she was trying to break free.

It made her question what it would take for Miguel to escape his past and think that a different future was possible for him. One that didn't end the way his mother's life had.

Maybe you, the little voice in her head said, but as Miguel dropped her off in his apartment after an FBI agent manned the door, she told herself that was impossible. She had dreams of an independent, adventurous life. One where she stood on her own and didn't need the protection of a man like Miguel.

But he could protect her from her father. From her past, and maybe that was part of the reason he intrigued her so. However, she wasn't ready to sacrifice all that she dreamed of. The sooner they could finish this investigation, the better it would be for both of them.

Which had her going back to the photos on her phone and her memories of the bomber in the hope of aiding in the investigation.

MIGUEL ENTERED THE BAU offices where Dash, Liam, and David were hard at work on their computers, digging up the information he had requested earlier.

Nicholas and Madeline were inside the large conference room, sitting kitty-corner to each other and poring over assorted papers. He wondered if they included information on Maisy and her father. He'd taken a moment away from her to text his team about what he'd discovered. Hopefully, whatever they had would confirm his gut reaction that Maisy had nothing to do with the bomber's actions.

He knocked on the door to the conference room and at Madeline's nod, he entered and sat. "What can you tell me?" He liked hearing what his team had to say before interjecting his own ideas into the investigation. He interrogated people much the same, letting them do the talking. It was amazing how much some criminals were willing to say voluntarily.

Madeline handed over a folder and as he opened it the face of an older white man stared back at him. Richard Green. Maisy's father.

He tried to find anything of her in him physically but decided she must take after her mother. As he read through the details, Madeline gave him a quick rundown.

"Richard Green, aka the Forest Conservation Bomber. Green had a successful landscaping business in Woodinville and was quite involved with local environmental groups, most of them legit. Somehow, he connected with the Forest Conservation League. Several of their members had been arrested for spiking trees, monkey-wrenching and arson. Green escalated their tactics to include over a dozen bombings at various logging locations and at a new construction site."

"Hug a tree, kill a human," Nicholas said with disdain.

"Extremism of any type can turn deadly," Miguel added, thinking of the many radical groups he'd handled during his counterterrorism activities.

"Maisy and her mom—" he began, but Nicholas beat him to it as Madeline handed him another folder, this one with photos of Maisy and her mother.

"Maisy was formerly Elizabeth Green. Her mother's maiden name was Patricia Kelly. Both her parents were only children, like Maisy. Maisy really has no other family except her father. Maisy and her mother have lived in Seattle since Green's imprisonment. Patricia was sickly for the last three years of her life before she passed from uterine cancer. From what we can see, Maisy was a dutiful daughter and took care of her mother."

Miguel nodded and peered at the photos of Patricia Oliver that his team had gathered from the DMV and news articles published during Richard Green's trial. She'd been a beautiful woman and it was obvious where Maisy got her looks. But the last photo of her from the DMV showed the ravages of illness and the difficult times she and Maisy must have suffered after escaping to Seattle.

The photos of a young Maisy were as telling. The teen had clearly been overwhelmed by all that had happened during the trial. She'd been sad and fearful based on her face and body language in the photos.

"What do you read from all this?" he asked his team.

"Your mother's profile and physical evidence gathered at various locations led to his capture at the landscaping business. Green didn't put up a fight when the agents showed up to arrest him, maybe because he was clearly guilty. No doubt about that, but he refused to cooperate about whether anyone else in the Forest Conservation League had assisted in any way," Madeline said.

"I doubt he acted alone, although he could have. Being in the landscaping business, he had access to everything he needed to build his bombs. Fertilizer. Fuel. That was his MO and that's nothing like what we have here," Nicholas said.

"If you're wondering about Maisy and her mother, they seem to have been terrorized by the press, neighbors and possibly even Green," Madeline added.

Miguel quirked a brow and closed the folders. "If I'm hearing you right, you don't think Maisy had any role in the bombing. Is that correct, Madeline?"

Madeline tipped her head and glanced at Nicholas, who likewise nodded and said, "I concur. If anything, Maisy and her mother were suffering from a form of PTSD based on what I see in the file. They've been doing all they can to avoid anything to do with the trauma. They changed their names and basically hid from the world. Now Maisy has suffered another trauma very reminiscent of the crimes her father committed. I wouldn't be surprised if she has nightmares or hypervigilance after that event."

Relief slammed into Miguel that his two profilers felt Maisy wasn't involved with the bomber, but he worried about the possible trauma that both his father and Maisy had suffered that day. And he also worried that the bomber wasn't done, which meant they had to work quickly to assist the local PD with a profile and anything that might help identify the bomber. Hopefully TEDAC could provide additional details once they'd examined the bomb remnants.

"Have you got anything on the profile for the bomber?" he asked.

Madeline and Nicholas shared an uneasy look before Nicholas quipped, "Besides that he likes ham sandwiches?"

Miguel had to chuckle. "Besides that. Although looking on the bright side, that likely eliminates Islamic extremists."

"It likely does. Plus, they would have claimed the attack already," Madeline said.

Miguel nodded and gingerly rose from his chair. His leg was throbbing, and other parts of his body were starting to chirp with pain from the bomb blast. "Excellent work on Green and Maisy. Keep digging to see if Green has any connection to this. Also, Maisy mentioned to me that she hadn't heard from her father for some time, but in the year since her mother passed, he's been terrorizing her with almost weekly letters and calls. Let's find out how he got Maisy's new name and info and see where that leads."

"Got it, boss," Nicholas confirmed.

"We've got this," Madeline added.

Satisfied that Nicholas and Madeline would glean additional information, he headed to the office area and over to Liam to see if he'd made any progress. As he neared, he noticed that Liam's attention was distracted for a moment as Lorelai offered a good-night to the group, almost glaring at Liam as she did so.

It had been a touchy situation in the office ever since the couple had called off their engagement, but Miguel couldn't let that interfere with this investigation.

"Liam, could I see you for a moment?" he said and tilted his head in the direction of his office.

Liam frowned, but nodded and hopped to his feet. As he entered the office, Miguel closed the door behind the young man, who took a seat in a chair in front of Miguel's desk. Miguel settled himself in his executive leather chair and stretched out his leg to ease the low throbbing there.

"You okay, boss?" Liam asked.

"Fine, and you, Liam? I imagine today must have been tough for you," he said, hoping to get the young man to open up.

"Not as tough a day as yours," Liam said, but then looked away and plowed on. "I nearly lost it when we heard from Lorelai that she was at the station.

All I could think about was whether she was safe. Whether I'd see her again."

"Seems to me you still have feelings for her," Miguel said, leaning his elbows on the arms of the chair and steepling his hands before his mouth. He gazed at Liam intently, trying to gauge what the young man was thinking.

"I do, but you know my family has a bad track record. I got cold feet and now… I promise I won't let this interfere with the investigation. If anything, I have lots more reason to find the bastard so that we can shut down any danger to the public or the team."

Miguel hesitated, carefully weighing Liam's words and tone. Satisfied that he was serious, he said, "Do you have anything for me?"

Liam nodded. "We constructed an image of his face that we're running against DMV and other agencies. David was able to pull a photo of him from a video, but also masked. Dash is working with those images using the facial recognition software he tweaked."

A knock came at the door and Miguel spied Dash there. As the top tech person, he oversaw Liam and David and so Miguel waved him in.

Dash's eyebrows issued a question he didn't ask, and Liam quickly said, "I just filled the SSA in on what we had so far. May I go back to work?"

Miguel nodded and Liam hurried back to his desk. Dash took Liam's spot and arched a brow. "Should my nose get out of joint that you went to Liam for a report?"

Miguel held his hands up in surrender. "No offense meant. I needed to make sure the Lorelai situation isn't out of control. I don't think it is, do you?"

Seemingly accepting the unspoken apology, Dash said, "It isn't. If anything, I'm betting we'll still be attending a wedding. How much did Liam tell you about our progress?"

With a heavy sigh, Miguel said, "That you have images you're running against various resources. I've sent you some photos that Maisy took. Don't know how helpful those will be."

"Quite. One of them contained a partial facial view. Part of the chin," Dash explained and used his hands to pinpoint the area that had been revealed by Maisy's photo.

"That's good news. When do you think we'll have a sketch to send to local PD, ABS and the other agents in our office?" Miguel asked.

"We should have a 3D rendering of the suspect's face as well as general physical characteristics by the morning. In the meantime, we're running what we have for now just in case we get a hit."

"Good work. Send me everything as soon as you can. I'm going back to my apartment to review everything Nicholas and Madeline dug up, plus the surveillance videos of the bombing. Something's off and I need to put my finger on what," he said and stood.

"Will do, Miguel," Dash said.

Miguel took only a moment to make sure his team had loaded all their work to their network and, satisfied he had everything he needed, he headed to his apartment a few floors down from the BAU offices. As the elevator opened, he caught sight of the FBI agent guarding the door.

When he neared, he said, "We're good for the night. Get some rest and I'll see you in the morning."

The agent nodded and walked off, leaving Miguel staring at the door to his home.

Not that it felt much like a home, as Maisy had clearly seen. It was just a place to lay his head for some rest. A place to work when he needed the solitude he couldn't get in the BAU offices.

Not a home, but he had to admit that with Maisy there it felt different. It felt more domestic, especially as he entered and she was curled up on the couch, watching a television program.

"Hi," she said, her voice slightly husky. Eyes half-closed, sleepy, until she saw him and beamed him a smile.

"Watching anything interesting?" he asked and walked over. He couldn't fail to notice it was a show about counterterrorism.

"It is. Scary as well when you think about how many plots you've stopped," she said and patted the space beside her.

He slipped off his suit jacket, folded it and laid it on a nearby chair. He sat down beside her, loosened his tie and undid his top two buttons of his shirt. Staring at the screen, he recognized the case that the show was highlighting—a German operation where it had seemed like a lone-wolf attack until additional ties to Al-Qaeda had been revealed. He explained to her and she listened intently, asking questions and shutting off the program to focus on him.

As he finished, she said, "That's fascinating. So what the FBI, NSA and CIA communicated to the Germans was able to stop a bigger attack?"

"It was. Much like we've gotten critical information from others, like the British police advising us about a possible transatlantic aircraft plot. It created a number of immediate security measures regarding liquids on flights and eventually we caught the terrorists before they could hurt anyone."

"It's why you're so married to what you do," Maisy said.

He'd never thought of it that way, but it was very similar to being married. To being committed to that one thing and not anything else. Not even a family.

"It's why my focus is on that and nothing else," he confirmed.

A long pause followed before Maisy cupped his jaw and gently urged him to face her. "It must be lonely. Being married to the job. Your mother wasn't that way."

"No, she wasn't. She was gone a lot, but she was also always there for me," he admitted.

Maisy stroked her thumb across his cheek, her touch soothing. Comforting. "I want to thank you for being here for me. I don't know what I would have done today after the bombing."

But he knew, because she'd shown him her true colors today and not just during the hostage situation. She'd shown him later with his dad and now, when she'd finally made his apartment feel like a home. When he'd shared his work with her, something he'd never done before with anyone.

"But *I* know. You'd have been strong the way you were today. The way you were when you and your mom built new lives for yourselves. You're a strong woman. A caring woman," he said and covered her hand with his. Stroked it to reciprocate the soothing and comfort she'd given him.

"Thank you. I only wish I was as strong as you, but promise me one thing," she said and paused until he nodded. "Promise me you'll stay safe. *¡Cuidate!*"

Somehow the promise took on new meaning with her. A challenging meaning because he could already imagine hearing that from her every morning. Could imagine coming home to Maisy.

And that was possibly more risky than the bomber who was on the loose.

"I promise," he said and rose from the sofa carefully, mindful of the stitches in his leg. He had stopped using the cane because the pain had lessened and the doctor had said to only use it when he felt he needed support. "Time for rest. I'll take the couch."

She shook her head and said, "You take the bed." She paused then and stared around the spacious studio apartment. "There is a bed, right?"

He gestured to the wall at one side of the room,

opposite a small dining room table and chairs. "Murphy bed. Are you sure?"

"You're a big man," she said and bright color flooded her cheeks. She hid it, rather unsuccessfully, by covering them with her delicate hands.

"You're cute when you're flustered," he said, smiled and playfully tapped her nose.

She mimicked the gesture. "And you're kind of handsome when you smile."

Heat filled his cheeks and he stopped himself from taking the flirting—*whoa, flirting*—to another level. "Good night, Maisy. Feel free to use the bathroom to change."

"Thanks," she said, grabbed her bag and hurried to the bathroom, but even as she did so, he couldn't stop smiling.

Armed with that smile, he rounded up a pillow, sheets and a blanket for Maisy. Yanked down the Murphy bed for himself. As he did so, he calculated the distance from the bed to the couch. Barely a few feet away. Too close and yet not close enough because it was too easy to picture her slipping into bed with him.

He suddenly wished that he had opted for a one bedroom instead of the studio because even those few feet would have lessened the temptation of having Maisy close by. In just a day she had touched his heart in ways no one had in a long time. He had to guard against that because he couldn't afford any distractions during this investigation.

The only damage the bomber had done so far had been to a building. Miguel intended to keep it that way. When Maisy came out, looking fresh-faced in her cotton pajamas, he bid her a terse good-night and escaped to the bathroom, determined to get his guard up.

When he exited, she was tucked beneath the blanket on the couch, all the lights off except for one under-cabinet light in the kitchen she'd thoughtfully snapped on.

He rushed to the bed and eased beneath the covers. Grabbing his laptop from a nearby table, he pulled up the files for the information they had so far. But his mind was only half on the work. The other half was on Maisy's gentle breathing until it lengthened and grew more regular, confirming that she had finally fallen asleep.

It was only then that he could focus on the investigation. His one hope was that they would catch the bomber quickly to avoid any more damage to the people and city of Seattle. No, make that two hopes: the second was that Maisy would be out of his life before he got any more attached to her.

Chapter Six

Maisy had lingered on the couch, feigning sleep, when Miguel had risen from bed with the first rays of the sun coloring the dawn. She'd heard him padding around in bare feet, opening drawers and a closet before heading to the bathroom, where the hiss of water in the pipes said he was showering. She told herself not to think about what he might look like dripping wet in the shower because this time together was limited and could go nowhere. They each had their own path to take and they would never meet again.

Determined to avoid those thoughts, she dressed, folded the sheet and blanket, and made a pot of coffee. The first drips of earthy brown java were filling the carafe when Miguel's phone started chirping angrily. It stopped for a second, but then started up again, warning her that something important was up.

Her instincts were confirmed when Miguel raced out of the bathroom, hair wet, dress shirt and pants unbuttoned, displaying the lean and toned muscles of his chest and midsection.

She looked away and busied herself with pouring a cup of coffee as he snatched up his phone and answered.

"SSA Peters," he said as he dragged a hand through his wet hair to smooth the longer strands at the top of his head.

The muffled words coming across the phone dragged a muttered curse from him and he grabbed the remote for the television and snapped it on. A "Breaking News" chyron in bright red and white scrolled across the screen.

"An explosion rocked a vacant apartment building in West Seattle this morning. Firefighters are at the location tending to a small blaze ignited by the blast. We're waiting for additional information as to the cause of the explosion and whether it has any connection to yesterday's terrorist bombing in King Street Station," the female newscaster reported as video of the firefighters tackling the fire flashed across the screen along with police officers securing the location.

"You're saying that the bomber sent a communication to us at the same time as the blast?" Miguel asked, his gaze focused on the news report as he listened to what one of his team members was reporting. He nodded at whatever they said and advised, "I'll be there in five. Start tracing who sent the email and get on social media. I have no doubt he'll be rubbing our faces in it on there as well."

He swiped to end the call and glanced at her as she said, "Is it him? The bomber from yesterday?"

He nodded again and said, "He's calling himself the Seattle Crusader. He says government isn't doing enough for the people of Seattle and so he's decided to help move things along. His first demand is that the minimum wage be increased to twenty dollars per hour. If we don't meet that demand, he'll keep blowing up parts of the city."

Maisy shook her head in disbelief. "But that's not even something that anyone can do right away."

"It isn't, but at least it's something. Not like what we had yesterday. Hopefully the team can trace the email so we can pinpoint where he might be. I need to get to work," he said and snapped off the television. "I'll send an agent down—"

"I'm going with you," she said and set aside the cup of coffee she had just poured.

"No way, Maisy. We'll be way too busy—"

"But you promised you'd be the one to safeguard me. And maybe I can help out somehow. Maybe I can remember something more about the bomber or what I remember of my dad, his trial and stuff," she said and tilted her chin up, almost daring him to refuse her request again.

A half smile slipped onto his lips. "Stuff, huh? I guess I'll be able to focus better if you're with me, even if I know any of my agents could protect you capably."

"For sure. I guess you should finish dressing," she said and gestured to his unbuttoned clothing, ignoring the rush of heat to her face and throughout her body as she looked at him again.

He coughed uncomfortably, slipped his smartphone into his pocket and immediately buttoned his shirt and pants, a stain of color on his cheeks as well. As he stuffed the shirt into his pants, he said, "There are to-go mugs in the middle cabinet." Apologetically, he added, "Please. Light and lots of sugar."

"No problem," she said and prepped two coffees as he finished dressing, made the bed and eased it back into the wall.

MIGUEL IGNORED THE questioning glances as he walked into the BAU offices with Maisy in tow and introduced her to the team sitting around the table in front of their board.

"Maisy Oliver. Please meet my BAU Team. Special Agent Madeline Striker. Her specialty is kidnapping cases. Special Agent Nicholas James is our go-to guy for serial killers. Special Agent Dashiell West is our cybercrimes and tech hotshot." He paused and gestured to the two younger men sitting off to the far side of the office, diligently working on their computers. "You'll get to meet Liam McDare and David Dyson later. They're our tech gurus."

A slight cough interrupted him, and he glanced toward the door leading to his director's private offices. "So sorry, Lorelai. How could I forget you? Lorelai Parker, the administrative assistant to Director Branson, who is in D.C. right now."

"And who is on the phone with Caitlyn Yang about this morning's bombing," Lorelai said, walked over and handed Miguel some message slips. "Caitlyn is coordinating with Seattle PD, ATF and Mack at ABS. They should have more info for you shortly."

Miguel nodded and at Maisy's questioning gaze, he said, "Caitlyn is our liaison with local law enforcement. Thank you, Lorelai."

As Lorelai walked out of the room, Liam's head swiveled to watch her walk to her office and Miguel once again worried about whether their personal drama would interfere with the BAU's efficiency. Which reminded him they had to get working on the latest bombing. Turning to Maisy, he said, "Please have a seat." Then he glanced toward his team and added, "What have we got so far?"

"A demand, finally. There's a new Twitter account for someone calling themselves the Seattle Crusader." Madeline hit a button to turn on an overhead monitor that projected an image of the Crusader's profile with its Twitter thread about the bombing. The first tweet said:

Shaking up Rat City until the politicians listen to our demands.

"'Rat City…our demands.' What's that telling us?" Miguel tossed out for consideration.

Dash's fingers flew across the keyboard and seconds later, he said, "Rat City is possibly a giveaway that he's local. It's a reference to the White Center.

Used to be a dump there with lots of rats, and also a hangout for sailors. Water rats was slang at one time for sailors."

Miguel went to the whiteboard and wrote down the word "local" under the grainy picture of the bomber tacked to the board.

Madeline added, "'*Our* demands.' It hints at the fact that the bomber is not working alone."

"So we may be dealing with a terrorist cell and not just an individual bomber," Miguel said and wrote that down on the board. "What else?"

Nicholas gestured to the second tweet in the thread and read it aloud. "No peace until the minimum wage is twenty dollars per hour."

"'No peace.' He's co-opting part of the call for social justice," Madeline noted and continued. "It could mean he's been involved with other groups using that phrase."

Miguel nodded, added the language beneath the photo and glanced at Dash. "Can you get us a list of anyone arrested during the riots after the bombing yesterday? By the way, how are we doing on the footage from the bombing at the station?"

MAISY LISTENED INTENTLY as Dash reported on the progress they'd made with the images from the CCTV in and around the station, Maisy's photos and the news crew videos. With a few strokes of his keyboard, he added a map to the image already being projected against the screen and as he spoke, he added pins to the map.

"We have the first bombing in the station and now this morning's blast near the White Center. The feeds we were able to access helped us track the unsub as he passed Century Link and T-Mobile fields and entered the SoDo area. We lost him there but are now working on getting video feeds from the area around the latest bombing location."

Miguel nodded, jotted down some notes on the board while Dash continued with his report. "As for the images, we've got a composite thanks to Maisy's photo. It let us add more detail to the bomber's face and we're running that composite against various databases and hope to have something shortly."

"Good work. Nicholas, what can you add now that we've got a serial bomber happening?" Miguel prompted.

"Two early-morning bombings, although I'm still bothered by the second bomb that exploded at King Street Station. It's off, Miguel. Totally off. Can you run that video for us, Dash?"

Dash did as Nicholas asked, putting up the CCTV feed. As it ran, Nicholas said, "We all thought the bomber looked surprised when that second bomb went off. Now we have 'our demands.' Maybe the reason he's surprised is that he wasn't the one who set off that second bomb. Maybe his partner tripped it before the bomber expected."

"Or maybe the bomber didn't expect for any bomb to go off," Madeline proposed. "We had no real demands despite that being the typical MO for the kind of collar bomb that was used. This morning we have another bombing, but I've done some digging and it turns out that the building that was blown up this morning was vacant and slated for destruction."

"We have another situation where the bomber chose a location that would do little collateral damage," Miguel said.

Unlike my father, Maisy thought. Her father had picked his targets to cause damage, both to the locations and any innocent passersby. "He doesn't want to hurt anyone," she said aloud, drawing the attention of the team members. "Or he's just been lucky. Even if the building was supposedly vacant, there could have been someone homeless there. Or one of the firefighters could be injured."

"But he didn't choose locations which would definitely cause injury like the Forest Conservation Bomber," Madeline said and eyed Maisy intently. "It's the eight-hundred-pound elephant in the room and I'm sorry to bring it up, Maisy. But it had to be said."

"It does, but I want you all to understand that my mother and I knew nothing about what he was doing," she pleaded, disheartened that she had to defend herself yet again after so many years.

To her surprise, Miguel walked over and laid a hand on her shoulder in reassurance. "We believe you, Maisy. And we get that you've been living in a prison much as your father has been, thanks to his actions."

Every member of the team peered at his hand on her shoulder, but no one said a thing about it.

"You're suffering every bit as much as one of his victims," Nicholas said. Then he quickly added, "And you're right that even if this bomber doesn't intend harm, there's no guarantee that no one will be injured or worse."

The phone in the center of the table chirped and Miguel leaned over to answer the call. "SSA Peters here."

"Miguel, it's Mack. I've got some info for you."

"You're on speaker with the team and Maisy Oliver, the young woman from the station yesterday," Miguel said.

"I wish I could say 'Good morning', but it isn't. Another bombing without a doubt. Initial review of the bomb fragments by ATF and me lead us to believe it was constructed much like yesterday's briefcase bomb. Tripped by a cell phone. The dynamite appears to be the same make as well. Blue wires again. We're in the process of trying to locate DNA samples and fingerprints. We'll keep you posted."

"Thanks, Mack. We're working on a profile as we speak and will fill you in as soon as we have anything," Miguel said and disconnected the call.

"A serial bomber, but again, a different MO between the collar bomb and the use of the dynamite. That's unusual, but it could confirm that we have two or more people working together," Nicholas said.

"And we have two very different locations. The

very public and crowded King Street Station and now an apartment building that's abandoned and soon to be destroyed," Madeline tossed out for consideration.

"Not really, Madeline," Nicholas interjected. "The second bomb in the station was in a little-used area. You might even say an abandoned area. Again, no harm intended."

"Terror was intended and now it's our job to trap this terrorist before he strikes again," Miguel pointed out.

And creates even more psychological harm, Maisy thought.

"Let's get to work on the building. Dash, can you find out who owns it? Why that might have made it the bomber's target. Also, to the best of my knowledge blue wire is mostly used in commercial buildings. Let's find suppliers in the area," Miguel said.

"On it," Dashiell confirmed, grabbed his laptop and headed to a desk near the two techies.

Miguel looked at Madeline and Nicholas. "The demand. Unreasonable. Nothing we can really do to fulfill it. Why? Does he really want those demands fulfilled or is it just a smoke screen for something else?"

Madeline nodded and glanced at her teammate. "Nicholas and I will work on it. I think we all agree something is very off about this bomber and hopefully we can work up a profile that gets us closer to understanding his motivation so we can prevent another bombing."

"Great. I look forward to hearing anything you can put together," Miguel said and looked at Maisy. "Would you mind joining me in my office?"

Chapter Seven

Maisy shook her head. "Not at all."

She rose and he held his hand out in invitation. She slipped her hand into his and followed him to his office. Unlike his very sterile apartment just a few floors down, this room was filled with bits of his life. As she sat, she tried to piece all those bits together to get a better picture of the man who was intriguing her on too many levels.

A bookcase behind the desk held an assortment of subjects. History. Psychology. Forensics. Crime. Some literature. Propping up the books, knickknacks from all over the world. A replica Aztec sun stone in gleaming black obsidian. Well-handled maracas painted with an age-muted floral design and the word "Cuba." A few different crystal beer steins that brightened the heavier objects on the shelves.

The walls were not as eclectic, more formal. Pictures of the BAU team with assorted politicians. Miguel shaking the hand of the President as he accepted an award. But the picture on his desk was purely personal. One of him with his father and a woman she assumed was his mother.

The desk was otherwise scrupulously neat and organized, like his apartment.

"Maisy?" he said, and she realized he had asked her something that she hadn't heard because she was so lost in her thoughts.

"I'm sorry. I didn't mean to ignore you," she said and leaned forward in her chair to make sure he knew that he had her complete attention.

He arched a brow. "I asked if you wanted some more coffee."

"No, thanks. I'm already jumping out of my skin, trying to process everything that's happening," she said and clasped her hands in her lap to tame her nervousness.

MIGUEL UNDERSTOOD. HE was always like that during the course of an investigation, his mind racing with all the facts they had and searching for all the ones they didn't.

"I get it. You feel like you're on a knife-sharp edge, barely keeping your balance. Waiting for what's coming next while hoping you can stop it," he said.

"You don't think he's done," she said and wrung her hands.

He shook his head. "Sadly, I think he's just getting started. And it is a he. Most serial bombers are men, like the Unabomber and Eric Rudolph, the Olympic Park Bomber. Your father."

"You mean the Forest Conservation Bomber. My father died the day that killer was born," she said, her voice alive with pain.

He nodded, in sync with her emotions, especially considering how Richard Green had terrorized Maisy in addition to the residents of Washington State. "In some ways, you're not wrong. With a bomber like your…like Green, they become consumed with what they're doing. With the building of the bombs and placing them. With the justification of what they're doing, whether it's protecting the environment or railing against technology."

"And this bomber. What do you think is his justification?" Maisy asked.

Miguel frowned and leaned back in his chair. Jammed his elbows on the arms of his chair and steepled his hands in front of him for a long moment. "That's what's bothering me about this bomber. The demands so far are unrealistic. Is that because he really doesn't want to stop bombing? Or is it for some other reason, especially since the locations of the bombs suggest an intent not to harm anyone?"

Maisy was likewise silent for a moment. "Unlike the Forest Conservation Bomber. He wanted to hurt people."

"Maybe as revenge for what he saw as damage to the environment. Revenge is often a motivation as well," Miguel said, but a second later his phone rang, snagging his attention as he saw the call was from his team in the conference room.

He picked it up, scowled and opened his desk drawer to remove a remote control for the television on one wall of his office. As he flipped on the television, he said, "I got it. Putting you on speakerphone."

Maisy swiveled in her seat and they watched the television, where the reporter was breaking news about another bombing at a construction site in the SoDo section, almost halfway between the original bombing site in King Street Station and that morning's blast near the White Center.

"He's already claiming this one," Madeline said.

Nicholas chimed in, "The Seattle Crusader just tweeted that he'll stop once the city council sets up a permanent homeless encampment on the grounds of the Seattle Japanese Garden. In the second tweet in the thread, he warns that next time people will feel the wrath of his bombs. Maybe even Angel Eyes."

Fear ripped through his gut at the mention of Maisy. If the bomber was still fixated on her like that, she was in even greater danger. "Dash, do you have anything yet on the account?" Miguel said.

Dash immediately replied, "We're still trying to get Twitter to give us info. Subpoena has been served on them so we're hoping to have it soon."

"But not soon enough," Nicholas said, concern ringing in his tone. "He's escalating. One bombing yesterday. Two today, just hours apart, and now he's threatening harm."

To Maisy, Miguel thought, and glanced her way.

Her face had gone chalk white at the bomber's mention of her. His gut clenched again at the thought that the bomber's threats were possibly no longer empty ones.

"And we still don't have demands that anyone can really meet," he tossed out, hoping to hear what his team would think about those requests.

"Not a one," Madeline said. "That's not typical of an extortion-type bomber. And the foul-up on the detonator at the station makes me wonder just how mission oriented he is."

"Still no one hurt and I'm not sure he will go through with that threat," Nicholas said, but that only partially relieved some of Miguel's worry.

"Any info on the first construction site? Owner? Other info?" he said.

"We have an owner, but it appears to be a shell company. Trying to track the real owner," Dashiell said.

"Good job. Let's get info on the second construction site. Reach out to ATF, Mack and Seattle PD for anything they might have. It's too soon for TEDAC, but let's push them. Let them know we've got two more explosions."

As his team confirmed his orders, Miguel snapped off the speakerphone and glanced at Maisy, who had barely regained some pink to her cheeks. "He won't hurt you, Maisy."

She shook her head and clenched and unclenched her hands. "It's not me I'm worried about."

He acknowledged that with a slow nod and chastised himself. Even in the short time he'd known her, he should have recognized her worry would have been for others. Much like her worry the day before had been for his father and not herself.

"You're a brave woman, Maisy Oliver." The sort of woman who could handle the kind of life he led. If he wanted a woman, which he didn't.

She shook her head and a harsh laugh escaped her. "Not by choice. Sometimes I wish…" She looked away, but it was impossible for him not to see the shimmer of tears in her eyes.

He rose and walked over. Cupped her cheek and gently urged her to face him. "You wish for a normal life. One untouched by violence, but sadly, that's not the kind of life the two of us have been forced to live. It's how we handle it that defines us."

As a tear escaped, she swiped it away and said, "I want *my* life, Miguel. The life I dreamed of before my father stole it. I won't let this bomber steal it again."

He wanted to say, "That's my girl," only she wasn't and never would be. Much as Maisy had chosen what she wanted to do with her life, so had he and it didn't include a woman like Maisy. Or any woman for that matter.

"I won't either. Believe me. You're safe with me," he said and motioned to his desk. "I have to get to work."

"Don't let me stop you."

WHILE MIGUEL WORKED at his desk, presumably reviewing a variety of reports and information on what they had so far, Maisy slipped in earbuds and turned her attention to various news reports, both written and televised.

Over and over the reporters repeated the Seattle Crusader's tweets and showed photos of the damage done at the three different locations. Many of them also made note of the references to Angel Eyes, but luckily the BAU team had kept her name and photos of her from the press in order to safeguard her.

As it had occurred to Miguel and his team, it struck her that the spot destroyed at King Street Station, as well as today's two locations, had been fairly isolated. This was much different from the places her father had chosen. He had injured someone at almost every bombing site while, this time, thankfully no one had been hurt so far.

But for how long? she thought. Would this bomber escalate when his unreasonable demands could not be met?

The phone rang again, and Miguel picked it up and tucked the receiver between his ear and shoulder as he listened while continuing to work. He turned to face her and said, "Seattle ABS confirmed dynamite was used at this morning's location. The same kind as he used at the station. They're working at the second spot now, but initial inspections lead them to believe it was also dynamite. Blue wires again, which must be his signature."

She nodded, processing the info, but before she could say anything, Miguel rose and gestured for them to leave his office and join the team outside. The BAU members were gathered around the table and in front of their whiteboard with all the information they had gathered so far.

On the television, a newscaster was just finishing up with details of the bombing and had reached out to an on-location reporter stationed just outside the construction site that had been damaged.

"We're here with state senate candidate Richard Rothwell. Senator Rothwell—"

"Not Senator yet, Jessica," Rothwell said with a smarmy smile, hands held up to stop the young female reporter.

The reporter nodded and said, "You've just tweeted that politicians and the FBI are failing Seattle."

"They are totally failing the city and its people. It's been close to twenty-four hours since the first bombing and we've heard nothing from the BAU team. Now we have two more bombings without any progress, but I can work with them to move the investigation along."

"Over my dead body," Miguel said, and all the team members nodded in agreement.

"What do you think about the bomber's demands? Is that something local politicians should consider?" the reporter asked.

"Well, that's a little more complicated and my

team and I are reviewing it. As you can imagine, it's a fine line to walk when you're dealing with a terrorist, but we'll have something for you later today," Rothwell postured.

The young woman turned back toward the camera and said, "Well, there you have it. That was state senate candidate Richard Rothwell and as he said, we'll be hearing more from him later."

"Hopefully not," Nicholas said as Madeline snapped off the television.

MIGUEL COULDN'T AGREE MORE. He was about to address the team when Lorelai came into the room to advise that he had a call from Director Branson.

It was impossible to miss that tech guy Liam perked up when his ex-fiancée entered, and as she walked out, he said, "How are you doing?"

"Fine," Lorelai replied with a diffident shrug and walked out with Miguel following her to take the call privately.

Lorelai motioned for him to use the director's office and as he closed the door, the phone rang and he picked up.

"Good afternoon, Olivia. I'm assuming you've seen the initial reports we've sent you via email," he said, hoping to head off any discussion of Rothwell's appearance.

"I've done a preliminary review in between budget sessions, but as you can imagine, the news is non-stop reports on the bombings and Rothwell. Do you have anything new to report?" she asked. In the background he heard other voices, which said she was in between meetings.

"We just got confirmation from Seattle ABS that dynamite appears to have been used at all three locations and we're working on tracking the source, as well as the wire used. The demands so far are unrealistic, but luckily all the locations seem to be chosen so as to not injure anyone," he reported.

"But he's escalating and so is Rothwell," she said.

Which he hadn't failed to notice. "He is and we're going to have to handle Rothwell."

"Sooner rather than later, Miguel. I know you're working hard on this, but it's time you let the public know what you can and counter Rothwell's insinuations that you're not doing anything."

"But every second he takes away—"

"Is a second you could be using to solve this case, yes. But it's getting noticed in D.C. If we're going to get the funding we need to continue to help others, you're going to have to take the time to handle Rothwell." Her voice grew muffled toward the end and he heard her say, "In a minute," to someone else.

Miguel inhaled deeply and blew out a harsh breath. Dragging a hand through his hair in frustration, he said, "Understood, Olivia. I'll schedule a press conference for later today."

"Thank you, Miguel. I know you will get it done." She disconnected before he could say another thing, clearly juggling multiple tasks on behalf of their BAU team.

Just as he had to handle Rothwell, no matter how much he might not like it.

Replacing the receiver, he exited Olivia's office. "Lorelai, would you please contact Caitlyn and ask her to set up a press conference at four. I'll let her choose the location. I just need lead time to get there."

"Will do, SSA Peters," Lorelai said with a nod.

But before he left, he said, "You doing okay? That bombing yesterday must have been scary for you."

She hesitated and sucked in a breath. Held it before blurting out, "It was. It makes you think about what's important."

"It does. If you need to talk, we're all here. Some more than others if you know what I mean," he said, and she offered him a stilted smile but nodded.

"I know. Same here, Miguel."

He returned to where the team and Maisy were gathered, discussing the information they had so far. Instead of interrupting, he took a seat next to Maisy and sat back to listen, absorbing their details while formulating what to say to the press later.

In no time he had worked out what he would report, but before that, he intended to call Mack at ABS, the police chief and the mayor to give them a heads-up to what he would be saying at the press conference. Besides, it was time that BAU provide them with the information that they had so far.

Beside him Maisy sat patiently, but he worried that with something so personal because of her background, she might be suffering emotionally during the investigation. He laid a hand on her shoulder and gave a reassuring squeeze as he stood.

"You're all doing a great job so far. I want you to focus on finding out more about the ownership on today's locations. Likewise, the origin of the wire. My gut tells me we're going to find something there."

"On it," Dash confirmed.

"And we're finalizing our profile of the serial bomber, but I have to tell you that it's a tough one. We're still struggling with the motivation because those demands are so unreasonable," Madeline said.

"Almost as if he doesn't care if we satisfy them," Nicholas added.

"I agree. There's something else motivating him. Making *them* do this, because I don't believe he's working alone. See what the DNA and fingerprints we have so far can confirm about that," Miguel said.

"Got it, Miguel. Nicholas and I will work on that while Dash and his techs deal with the rest," Madeline advised.

"Great. Maisy and I are going to take a short break and prepare for the press conference," he said and with another gentle squeeze on Maisy's shoulder, he urged her to rise and head to his office for the preparation he had mentioned.

But as soon as they were inside the office, Maisy said, "Will I be at the press conference?"

It was something he'd been thinking about in addition to his statement to the reporters who would be there. In truth, he had been silently waffling about it.

"I know that you and your mother worked hard to avoid the public eye, so I have to ask, do you want to be there?"

Chapter Eight

Do I want to be there? she asked herself, but the answer came to her almost immediately.

"If you think it will help the investigation, I will be there."

His answer was not as immediate. After a long hesitation, he said, "I'm not sure it will help other than to let the bomber know we're protecting you. That could draw him out—"

"Then I will be there. I'm not afraid of him. I'm tired of being afraid," she said, thinking of how much time she and her mother had lost hiding out from her father. All for naught since her father had tracked her down anyway.

He stepped closer and cradled her cheek. "You're a unique woman. Don't ever change."

His touch sent comfort and need through her. It had been way too long, maybe never, since a man had looked at her like this. Touched her like this, and it was worrisome because it could upend her plans for what she'd wanted for so long.

She took a step back from him and wrung her

hands together because she was way too tempted to touch him back. To avoid it getting personal again, she said, "Do you think we could get some lunch? I'm kinda hungry."

In sympathy, his stomach rumbled, and he laid a hand over his lean midsection to quiet the noise. "Me, too."

Happy laughter and Liam's shout of "You rock, Lorelai," filtered into Miguel's office. They looked back toward the common space where the rest of the team was working and where it appeared that the ever-efficient administrative assistant had arranged for lunch to be brought in.

Miguel held his hand out in invitation. "I guess we should join them."

Maisy normally had trepidation about being with people, having avoided them for so long. But in just two short days, she'd grown comfortable with Miguel and his dad. Even with this group of FBI agents who had accepted her into their midst. Not an easy thing to do considering her family's history. In the back of her mind there was still doubt about their acceptance, but she wasn't going to let that keep her from helping them end the bomber's reign of terror.

They joined the team at lunch, but Maisy kept silent so she could listen and watch Miguel and the team members interact. It was clear Miguel was the person in charge and yet there wasn't any hint of competition or tension, except for possibly the whole

Lorelai-Liam situation. The tension there was obvious to everyone.

But the rest of the team seemed fluid and assured in their positions. It made her wish that she was as sure of her position in life. After all, she'd only just really begun her life by stepping on that bus yesterday, and then it had all come to a crashing halt. Or maybe it was more accurate to say it all blew up in her face.

Since she was surrounded by Miguel's team, however, hope filled her that this was only a bump in the road because she trusted that they would soon solve this investigation so she could get on with her life.

Lunch passed amiably, but as they were cleaning up and getting back to work, tension built inside her as the time neared for the press conference. With barely half an hour to go, Miguel got a call from Caitlyn with the location for the gathering.

"I'm not sure that's a good idea," Miguel said and shot a quick look at her.

She couldn't hear what the team's liaison said, but Miguel was clearly unhappy with whatever plan was in place. Despite that, he said, "I hope you're right."

He swiped to end the call and peered at her intently. "The press conference is going to be at the site of this morning's bombing. We'll be taking along other agents to secure the area, so you'll be safe."

She peered at him, trying to read him since he was clearly not happy with Caitlyn's choice. "But you're not in favor of the location, are you?"

He scowled and shook his head. "Not one hundred percent. There are too many variables in such a public place, but as I said, we'll have other agents there for security. That's my main concern."

She appreciated that, but more importantly, she had total confidence in him and his team.

She laid a hand on his arm and said, "I trust you. I guess we should get going."

As he had before, he cradled her cheek, offering reassurance with that simple touch. "Thank you for that trust. I just need a few minutes to get a team together to secure the area and then we'll head over."

Instead of stepping away, she cupped her hand with his and said, "Whenever you're ready, I'm ready."

MIGUEL'S TEAM OF agents had gone ahead to secure the space and at their signal, he and Maisy drove to where a number of news teams were gathered in front of the vacant apartment building that had been slated for destruction even before the actions of the Seattle Crusader.

As their car pulled up, Miguel noticed that besides the news crews, there were also quite a few of what appeared to be demonstrators gathered at the location. Using the headset he was wearing, he instructed his team. "Get photos of everyone in the crowd. It's possible the bomber has come back to check out his handiwork."

A second later, a knock on the glass had him looking into Caitlyn's worried features. He opened the door, stepped out and then helped Maisy from the car. "I guess someone leaked the location of the press conference," he said to the BAU liaison.

"I'm so sorry, SSA. You were right that this area would be hard to keep quiet," Caitlyn said.

"It's okay. We can handle this," he said, took hold of Maisy's hand and guided her to a spot to the side of where various microphones had been placed before a sea of videographers and photographers from the local papers and television news. An agent stood there, hands folded in front of him and at his nod, Miguel guided her to the agent.

"You'll be okay here," he said and at her nod, he and Caitlyn walked up to the microphones.

Shutters clicked and reporters jockeyed for positions as Caitlyn began the press conference.

"Good afternoon. I'm Caitlyn Yang, the BAU liaison. I have with me Supervisory Special Agent Miguel Peters, who is leading the team investigating the bombings that have taken place at King Street Station, the location behind us and the construction site in SoDo."

"You mean the Seattle Crusader, don't you?" someone shouted.

Miguel decided it was as good a time as any to take control of the press conference. "The individual we are investigating has named himself the Seattle Crusader. My team has received information from local authorities and is working on our profile of the bomber, as well as interacting with other agencies."

"But are you any closer to catching him?" a too-familiar voice called out from the crowd as Richard Rothwell moved to the front of the gathering and all cameras shifted in his direction.

Before anyone could stop him, Rothwell took a spot beside Caitlyn and continued. "As I said earlier, I am more than prepared to work with the FBI in order to capture this individual. But in the meantime, why aren't we considering some of his demands? For example, since the suspect is demanding the government up the minimum wage to twenty dollars per hour, let's meet him in the middle and give the good people of Seattle seventeen dollars! You all deserve more, don't you?"

While the press conference was happening, the number of people had grown and after Rothwell finished, a crowd of supporters, probably paid to be there, cheered and held up campaign signs with his name.

Miguel waited for the cheering to die down somewhat and said, "Thank you, *Mr.* Rothwell. While we appreciate the offer of assistance, my team has this under control."

"But do you?" Rothwell challenged, pompously puffing out a chest covered with the vest of a pin-striped suit. "I have a number of connections in government who could assist—"

"And I appreciate the offer, but as I said, we have

this under control. We're interfacing with various agencies both here and in D.C. We'll have more information from them shortly and will be offering our complete profile to ATF, Seattle PD and ABS within hours. Additional investigations are ongoing to pinpoint the origin of the materials used in the bombings. Finally, we believe the bomber is not acting alone and will provide additional information on this conspiracy within twenty-four hours."

Miguel didn't fail to notice Rothwell's reaction to that statement. The man did a little jump, and his face paled. It sent up a red flag and as wild as it might be, his gut told him that Rothwell's involvement in this might be about more than the campaign.

Replacing his obvious discomfit with bluster, Rothwell said, "I can assure you that we're all looking forward to your report, Agent Peters."

Tired of the man and his interruptions, he said, "That's Supervisory Special Agent Peters, *Mr.* Rothwell. Now if you'll excuse me, we have bombers to catch."

He didn't wait for any questions, leaving Caitlyn to wind up the press conference and forward any pertinent questions to him at his office. To the side of the space, he joined Maisy and the agent guarding her, who walked them to the car waiting to return them to the BAU offices.

As soon as they were seated and on the way, Maisy said, "You said 'bombers.' I know your team was tossing that out, but are you sure?"

He thought about it for a hot second and nodded. "The team put it out there for discussion after the Crusader's tweets. My gut tells me we're not wrong going that route. This bomber isn't acting alone. Which reminds me…"

He took out his phone and dialed Caitlyn. "Sorry for leaving you to the wolves."

"No, I deserve that. You were right about the location," the young woman said again.

"And as I said, no problem. But I need something from you and your connections," he said.

A resigned sigh came over the line before Caitlyn said, "Anything. What can I do?"

"Anything and everything you can get me on Rothwell. The man. His businesses. Who's feeding him information." He kept to himself that he felt that Rothwell always seemed to be one step ahead of them, but maybe that was because Rothwell knew more about what was happening than he let on. That maybe he was somehow involved with the bombings.

"You got it, Miguel. I'll try to round up what I can by later tonight and will send it to you," Caitlyn said and hung up.

"You think Rothwell is part of this, don't you?" Maisy asked.

"I have no proof, but I think it's worth exploring. How about you?" he asked and stared at her, trying to gauge her reaction.

She wrinkled her nose and pursed her lips—full lips he had trouble ignoring—and said, "I agree. He just rubs me the wrong way. And how come he's always there like a Johnny-on-the-spot."

"And stinks like one, too," he teased, prompting a smile from her.

"For sure. What do we do now?" she said.

He liked that she said "we" because it was a team effort, including her. "We go back to work."

MAISY SAT AND listened as the BAU team reviewed what they had gathered in the short time they were gone to do the press conference. Unfortunately, it appeared that they had hit a dead end at getting any information about who had opened up the Twitter account.

"The email used to open the account is fake and was created just an hour before at a computer at the local library. No CCTV inside the library and we've had Seattle PD dust for fingerprints, but the computer was used by multiple people since then. Liam is searching for any CCTV feeds in the area of the library," Dashiell noted.

"And there was no sign-up for the computers. They could be used by anyone at any time. No one remembers anything out of the ordinary. We've sent agents to the homes of the librarians on that floor, as well as the security guard, with the initial photo that Dash and his team created. Still waiting to hear from them," Madeline indicated.

"Good. Hopefully, it might trigger a memory. Do

we have anything else from ABS on the explosives or other evidence?" Miguel asked.

"Dynamite again. Looks like the same batch that was used at the station. The blue wires again. TEDAC is analyzing the bomb materials and in the meantime, David is working on getting a list of any licensed blasters in the area who might have access to that kind of explosive as well as the wire," Nicholas offered.

"And the DNA casework unit is analyzing the touch DNA samples taken from the briefcase handle and collar bomb. They should have something by tomorrow and run those results against CODIS," Dashiell added to the team's report.

It seemed as if they were covering all the bases so far, but what did she know? She was only a civilian drawn into this investigation. The crime was too painfully similar to what her father had done so many years earlier. Which made her wonder if there were other bombers like her father who were no longer imprisoned. Or maybe protesters who had used explosives. To her surprise Miguel, who had been mostly leaning back in his chair, listening to his team report, must have been thinking the same thing.

"I'd like to make a list of any possible unsubs who fit this profile. White. Above-average intelligence, but usually underachievers. Socially inept. Let's start with any known bombers or people on our terrorist watch list. Add to that any protesters arrested for using fireworks or other explosives. As for the DNA, when we get the results, let's check them against whatever genealogy databases we can access."

Madeline peered around the table at the team members and said, "We'll tackle that ASAP."

"I will as well," Miguel said and shot a quick glance in her direction. "In the meantime, I think we all could use a break. Go get something to eat. Take a walk. Clear your minds. I'm going to take Maisy for dinner and then head home to work. If anything pops up in the meantime, call."

"Got it, Miguel. I am ready for some food and a walk to clear my brain. Anyone want to join me?" Nicholas said and rose from the table.

"I'm game," Madeline said and likewise stood and stretched.

Dashiell glanced over his shoulder at where Liam and David were at their desks, still at work. "We have just a few things to finish up and then we'll meet you."

Miguel slowly unfolded from the chair, clearly favoring his one leg, reminding her that he was still recovering from an earlier wound. He winced as he took a step away from the table, but then schooled his features and forced a smile in her direction. Holding out his hand, he said, "Ready?"

"Yes," she said and slipped her hand into his. He squeezed her hand gently, offering comfort with his touch. Comfort that filled her and said that she could count on him, and his team, to end this threat to her and to the city of Seattle.

Together they walked out of the BAU offices and to the elevator, but once inside, he said, "There's a good fish place a block or so away if you'd like."

"Are you good to do the walk?" she asked, well aware of how gingerly he'd been moving.

"A walk will do me good. My leg stiffened up from sitting for so long, but it's almost healed," he admitted and pressed the elevator button for the lobby.

She wanted to ask how he'd been hurt but worried it would go down a road like that which his father had taken. That it was time for him to change his career, but Miguel intrigued her, and she needed to know what made him tick.

As the elevator moved toward the lobby, she said, "How were you hurt? If you can tell me, that is."

With a slight shrug, he said, "I can if you really want to know."

"I do. Before you my interactions with the FBI were…let's say not as pleasant," she said, recalling what had happened in the days and weeks after her father had been identified as the Forest Conservation Bomber.

"Apologies for that, but I hope you understand that we have a job to do to protect people," he said.

The elevator doors slid open noiselessly, spilling them into the pristine lobby of the building. Still hand in hand they stepped out and across the lobby filled with workers leaving for either dinner or the night after a long day. Outside the weather was unseasonably warm for an October night, making for a pleasant walk to the restaurant just a couple of blocks from the skyscraper where Miguel worked and lived.

After they were seated, she returned to their earlier conversation, which they'd set aside to enjoy the beauty of the fall night.

"Do you mind sharing how you were hurt? What the case was about?"

She needed to know what made him give up any kind of personal life to protect people like her. Maybe by knowing that, she could battle her growing attraction to the handsome FBI agent. Sitting back in her chair, she waited for him to answer.

Chapter Nine

Miguel delayed, unsure of where the discussion would go if he told her. Hopefully not to where such discussions usually went with his father.

"We had identified the unsub…" He stopped at the puzzled look that slipped across her face at his use of the term.

"I've heard that used, but what does it really mean?" she asked.

"Unknown subject. It's the person or persons who are unidentified and the focus of our investigations. Just easier to say unsub," he replied with a smile and shot a quick glance at the menu. Well familiar with it since the restaurant was a favorite, he immediately knew what he would order.

"Totally easier. So you had identified the unsub," she prompted and also took a look at the menu.

He nodded. "We had cornered him when he opened fire. I was shot during the confrontation, but we were able to capture him. My team and I got the job done."

"That's important to you, isn't it? That it's the

team that accomplished it," she said, acutely in tune with him, which pleased him.

"It's a team effort. Everyone on the team contributes to the end result. If one person is off, it could impact the efficiency of the team."

"Which is why you're worried about Lorelai and Liam," she said just as the waitress came over to take their orders.

"The salmon, please," Maisy said.

"The same and a bottle of the sauvignon blanc," Miguel said and immediately returned to the conversation. "It worries me because of the effect on the team, but also because I think they'd be very happy together."

"I can't argue with you. They seem to still care for one another despite the obvious tension," Maisy said and added, "Tell me about the rest of the team."

Miguel didn't hesitate to offer up his observations of the other team members and each of their respective specialties.

Several minutes later, the waitress returned with a bottle of wine to uncork and pour it for them. When she stepped away, Maisy held up the glass and said, "To your team."

"To the team," he replied and sipped the wine. The taste was crisp in his mouth, fresh with overtones of grass and a slight fruitiness.

"You care about your team being happy," Maisy said as she peered at him over the rim of the wineglass.

With a slight shrug, he said, "I do. In the last several months, many of the team members have found their significant others. It worried me at first since it happened during our investigations, but I see how much more centered they are and that's a good thing."

"But not you."

And there they were at that spot he hadn't wanted to reach like he did with his dad. "Not me. Not ever. When my mother and her partner were killed, I saw the pain that was left behind. My father. Her partner's wife and baby. A baby who will never know its father."

It had been painful for him as well to deal with those deaths. With the loss of his mother at the hands of a terrorist and its aftermath. It had only intensified his desire to follow in his mother's footsteps.

"That makes for a lonely life."

It was impossible to miss how she avoided his gaze by fixing it on the wineglass. It was likewise impossible to miss that the comment was also about her. About her life, and it made him sad.

"It was tough for you. You were so young, and people were cruel. And in a different way, you lost the father you knew and gained a monster. One who is tormenting you again," he said, but at that moment the waitress and another server came over with their meals. With almost artistic efficiency, the cedar-plank-cooked salmon was plated before them, along with an assortment of grilled vegetables.

Once they'd left, Maisy said, "I won't let him stop me from living. You shouldn't let your mother's death stop you either."

"It hasn't," he said, jabbed at a piece of salmon and shoved it into his mouth. Emotion made it tasteless since he hated to admit that Maisy might have a point.

MAISY COULDN'T MISS Miguel's upset, but she also couldn't say what was on her mind. For too long she'd held back because of the need to stay hidden to avoid the press and her father. Watching her mother slowly die before her eyes had only confirmed that it was time for her to reach for her dreams. To live. But happily, and to avoid any more unhappiness during the meal, she changed the topic.

"What was it like to grow up in Miami? It's probably very different from here."

He stopped shoveling food and met her gaze. The tension fled before her eyes, and a small smile quirked one side of his mouth. "Very. Tropical for starters. More diverse since there are so many different Latinos and other cultures."

"But your mom was Cuban?" she asked and forked up some asparagus from her plate.

He nodded. "She was born in Cuba and her family escaped Castro's regime in the early '60s. She loved this country. I think that's what made her join the FBI. She'd do anything to protect this nation."

"She sounds amazing," Maisy said with a sigh and sipped the last of her wine.

Miguel immediately refilled her glass. "Your mom must have been amazing as well to deal with everything that happened."

Maisy smiled. "She was. As difficult as it might have been, she tried so hard to give us a good life. It wasn't easy, but we had some happy times despite everything."

Nodding, Miguel finished the last bite of his salmon. "Once we're done with this investigation, you'll be able to go on with your life."

She didn't know why, but the prospect of that didn't make her as happy as she'd been only yesterday, when she'd set foot on the bus to start the rest of her life. Maybe because of Miguel. He had so many layers and so much pain, and something inside of her responded to that. Maybe too much.

When the waitress came by to ask about coffee and dessert, she demurred, aware that Miguel needed to get to work. Aware that she needed a little distance from him to deal with what she was unexpectedly feeling about him.

After they finished the bottle of wine and chatted some more about Miami, Miguel paid and they strolled back to the BAU office and his apartment, but even though it was a leisurely pace, she sensed that Miguel was on high alert. He swiveled his head slowly around to keep an eye out, making her wonder if he was taking the Seattle Crusader's threats toward her seriously.

"Do you think he'll come after me? Attack others?" she asked as they neared the door to his building.

"I won't let him hurt you. Or others," he said, laid a hand on her shoulder and gently squeezed.

To her surprise, she felt herself drifting toward him, stepping against him. He eased his arm around her shoulders to keep her there. Dropped the barest hint of a kiss on her temple.

She slipped an arm around him beneath his jacket, but as she did so, she brushed against the holster tucked beneath his suit. It jolted her, that reminder that they weren't ordinary people. That fate had thrown them together unexpectedly and would tear them apart much the same.

Because of that, she stepped back. "I guess it's time for you to get to work."

As HARD AS Miguel tried, his full attention kept on drifting away from his laptop to Maisy as she huddled beneath the covers on her makeshift bed.

It had been tense when they'd first gotten back from the restaurant, and he'd changed while Maisy showered. After, in silence, they'd slipped into their respective beds. Maisy had pulled out her tablet and slipped on headphones to watch something in deference to his need to work. Not that she'd needed to do that since he was used to working in utter bedlam and could usually focus without fail.

But not tonight. The more time he spent around her, the harder she was to ignore. And the harder it was not to imagine having her in his life more regularly. If she would have it, that was. She had her own plans for life, and he was sure they didn't include a relationship.

Like mine doesn't include one, he thought and returned to reviewing the initial list of terrorist suspects his team had identified. Satisfied with their choices, he went through those they hadn't chosen, but didn't find any to add at the moment. Except for one—Richard Rothwell.

Some might say it was his hubris driving him to dislike the politician, but he'd long ago learned to not let pride interfere with an investigation. He'd also learned to follow his gut and his gut was telling him that there was something off with Rothwell.

Because of that, he turned his attention to learning what he could about the politician and his background. And as he read, more and more pieces fell into place, convincing him that he wasn't barking up the wrong tree. The Seattle Crusader was parroting many of Rothwell's political stands, although taken to an extreme. That only made Rothwell's less progressive positions more palatable.

And Rothwell was heavily into real estate and construction. That meant someone at one of his active builds might have access to dynamite and wire. But so far, they only had shell companies owning the two bombing sites. His team was going to have to bust through those shells and see if they led to the blowhard politician.

He shut his laptop and sank down beneath his comforter, but as he did, a sharp cry of alarm drew his attention to Maisy.

She was restless, kicking away her blanket and sheets. The muscles in her arms twitched a second before one arm flailed out, as if pushing someone away.

Nicholas's comments about Maisy and her mother suffering from some kind of PTSD flashed through his brain. PTSD and nightmares like the one Maisy was clearly having.

He eased from his bed and approached her slowly, not wanting to scare her. As she swept her arm out again, almost tumbling herself from the sofa, she blasted awake and screamed at the sight of him. But as she realized it was him, she calmed, sat up and wrapped her arms around herself.

Her teeth were chattering as she said, "I'm sorry. I didn't mean to wake you."

He sat across from her and cradled her cheek. "I wasn't sleeping. Are you okay?"

AM I OKAY? Maisy asked herself and shook her head.

"It was a dream, but it was so real. My father...he was there, and bombs were exploding everywhere. My mom was with me and I was trying to protect her, but..." She couldn't finish because the vision in her mind was too extreme. Too scary.

Too alone, which made her lean toward Miguel, seeking his comfort.

Comfort he didn't fail to give.

He wrapped his arms around her and drew her into his lap. Held her against him as he murmured, "Your dad can't hurt you anymore. I'll make sure of that."

"I know," she said, hating how childlike she sounded. Much like she had sounded over a decade earlier, when the reality of her father's actions had come to light.

He surprised her then by exploding to his feet, cradling her in his arms and walking with her to his bed. "Miguel?"

"It's big enough for both of us," he said and laid her on the comforter.

She nodded and as he released her, she slipped beneath the sheets. He joined her a second later and as he had before, drew her into his arms, belying his comment that the bed was big enough.

It felt way too small with his hard body pressed to hers, but it wasn't just desire that filled her, but comfort. Safety. He was a rock. Her rock and she believed him when he said she would be safe.

Armed with that, the nightmare faded into the dark, replaced by a lightness in her soul created by his touch.

MAISY WAS STIFF in his arms at first, but the tension fled her body little by little and her breathing lengthened, confirming that she had fallen asleep.

But sleep didn't come as quickly to him, lying there beside her. Her lithe but strong body pressed to his, forcing him to tamp down unwanted desire. Desire that would only complicate even more the confusing thoughts he was having about her.

To keep those thoughts at bay, he turned his attention to what he'd been working on before Maisy's nightmare. The list of suspects. The dynamite. Wire. Locations. Rothwell. Rothwell. Rothwell.

Annoyance at the politician flared through him, which was good. It would keep him from thinking about Maisy's body. Her warm breath, toothpaste fresh, spilling across the skin of his chest. Her skin, smooth, so smooth along his.

He muttered a curse as desire flared to life again, but luckily, Maisy peacefully turned in his arms and shifted away from him.

Safe. He was safe, at least for tonight. And she was safe and that had to be what he focused on: keeping Maisy and Seattle safe.

He couldn't let anything else distract him.

Chapter Ten

Breath, hot against his neck. The brush of hair, silky smooth, along his chin. Her body, soft beside his hard, slowly awakening need from the night before.

He sucked in a slow breath and held it just as she did the same, and her softness tensed with awareness. Awareness of arms wrapped around each other and tangled legs as they undid their pretzelness and shifted toward the edges of the bed.

"Good morning," he said first, his voice morning rough. Or at least that's what he told himself.

"Good morning," she said and looked at her watch. "It's early. Not even six."

To which his phone alarm responded by blaring like a trumpet on steroids, warning that it was time to rise. From the bed, that was.

"I need to get going. You can use the shower first if you want."

She blinked twice, almost a crime because it hid her amazing blue eyes for those brief moments. With a quick lick of her lips, she said, "I showered last night. Remember?"

How could he have forgotten? Maisy coming out from the bathroom, steam chasing her. The smell of her lavender bath gel perfuming the air. Her face rosy cheeked from the heat of the water as she settled into bed with the tablet.

Get a grip, Peters! You're an FBI agent not a love-sick teenager, he told himself.

"Sure. Yes, I remember now. Sorry. I'll hit the shower and then we'll go to the office."

MIGUEL VIRTUALLY JUMPED *out of bed*, Maisy thought, recalling a rabbit she had scared out of a small vegetable garden her mother and she had planted at one of their rented homes.

With him gone and the susurrus of water running through the pipes, she likewise rushed from the bed, straightened it and then raised the Murphy bed back into the wall.

Grabbing some clothes from her suitcase, she quickly dressed and went to the kitchen to make some coffee. Feeling almost at home, she took the to-go cups from a cabinet. Grabbed half-and-half from the fridge and placed it beside the sugar canister on the counter.

Maisy had just finished making her coffee and was pouring his—light and lots of sugar—when he came out of the bathroom half-dressed.

And suddenly the heat she felt wasn't from the sip of hot coffee she'd taken. Dragging her gaze away from his unbuttoned shirt and the sculpted chest beneath, she turned her attention to prepping his coffee. Slowly scooping, pouring and stirring until he stood next to her, fully dressed.

"Ready?" he asked.

More than ready, she thought and nodded. "All set."

As he had yesterday, he laid a hand on her shoulder as if to guide her out of the apartment. He was a toucher, she'd learned in just the short two days since fate had tossed them together. And she kind of liked it because it was a comforting touch. A protective one.

In no time they were out and up in the BAU offices where his team was already at work. If it wasn't for the different clothes they were wearing, she might have thought that they had been there all night. But even if they had gone home, like Miguel they had probably spent the better part of the night reviewing the information for the case.

That was clear as Miguel stepped over to the board, greeted them and said, "What do we have today?"

Madeline popped up from her chair and handed out a sheet of paper to each team member. "Nicholas and I reviewed our watch list and have selected these terrorists as candidates for our possible unsub. We've also added our top candidates from those recently arrested in the riots."

Madeline sat and with a half glance at Nicholas, she tagged her team member to continue. "Each of these men fits our profile. They've all been either engaged in incidents involving explosives or violent political attacks. Our top candidate calls himself the Freedom Fascist. Real name Bob Smith. He's suspected of planting several IEDs at local police stations and the federal courthouse. Local PD had him in custody, but he was released thanks to new no-bail policies. Now he's gone to ground."

When Nicholas paused to hand out additional papers with the unsub's rap sheet and history, Miguel wrote his name on the board. But after, he said, "I'm not sold on Bob being our unsub."

Miguel's comment had the team all sitting higher in their chairs and glancing around at each other, making Maisy wonder if his challenge was sitting well with the team.

MIGUEL TOOK NOTE of his team's faces. Madeline's had paled slightly beneath her flawless brown skin. Nicholas's cheeks were ruddy, as if with embarrassment. Dash's face was hard, immobile. Only the drum of his fingers gave any hint to what he was feeling. Possibly nervousness.

"We ran through the lists over and over, Miguel," Madeline said.

"He fits the profile," Nicholas said.

"Almost too perfectly," Miguel replied and then gestured toward Maisy. "And don't let Maisy throw you from our usual routine. No one hits it out of the park the first time every time."

"Why do men always use sports metaphors?" Madeline mumbled, but with a smile.

"Because sports rock," Dash said with a laugh.

"They do and so does the work you did on this list. But like I said, I'm just not feeling Bob as our first choice. For starters, he's using M-80s and our unsub is primarily relying on dynamite. By the way, any luck on that front?" Miguel said and looked at Dash for an answer.

"Liam and David are running down lists of active construction sites and licensed master blasters at those sites. Also working hard on breaking past the shell on those shell companies. Trying to find the real owners."

"What about Rothwell and his companies?" Miguel pressed.

"Working on it. He's part owner of quite a few corporations and as you might guess, a lot of companies under them. Liam is compiling the list and I guess you're hoping we'll find a link."

"Or that we can completely eliminate him as a suspect. It's what we need to do. Examine every possible clue, and his turning up all the time is just too much coincidence for me. But let's get back to the list of candidates you worked up," Miguel said and went into listening mode like in his normal routine. Trying not to let Maisy change things up, just as he had asked his team to not let her presence change things.

But it was hard to do as she sat there silently but clearly engaged. It was obvious from the way her face reflected her thoughts. She had an expressive face. Eyes widening when she took in new information. Narrowing, as if in doubt, while they discussed another two of their suspects. A slight nod, later toward lunch, as despite his misgivings, they settled on Bob Smith, aka Freedom Fascist, as their primary unsub.

Like she had the day before, the ever-efficient Lorelai had arranged for lunch to be brought in, but as the food was laid out in the center of the table, Miguel excused himself and headed to his office.

They needed to find the Freedom Fascist and interview him. First thing was to reach out to Seattle PD and put out a BOLO on the man as a person of interest. Second was to contact some of his local informants and see if they were familiar with the man and if so, what information they could provide to either capture him, confirm he was the unsub or eliminate him as a suspect.

To his surprise, he hit gold with the second call. One of his informants, Joseph Michaels, was a former drug dealer turned pub owner with connections to the local antifascist movement. Miguel suspected that despite his claim to not be dealing, he was likely providing drugs to some in that movement.

"You know this guy?" Miguel asked.

"Not only know him, he was here in the pub having lunch just a few minutes ago. Had a few buddies with him and I overheard him talking about the bombings," Joseph said.

"I imagine he supports the bombings," Miguel said, thinking about the demands and how they fit the narrative some of the protesters were spouting.

"More than that. He was telling his buddies that he's the bomber and they were all congratulating him."

Miguel considered it for a second and with a shake of his head, he said, "Did you believe him?"

A choked laugh greeted his statement. "Dude, who knows. I mean, if you really did it, would you be bragging about it in public? But he sounded pretty convincing. Claimed he had a master blaster giving him the dynamite. That he was getting another bomb ready for tomorrow."

And if he was the unsub, that meant they needed to get him into custody. One of the points in their profile was that the bomber would strike again soon, and Joseph had just confirmed that was the Freedom Fascist's plan.

"Do you know where he and his friends were going?"

"They were headed over to the courthouse for another protest. If you're looking for him, he had a pig face mask in his pocket. Black hoodie, blue jeans and a bright red T-shirt."

"Thanks, Joseph," he said, and another laugh drifted over the phone line.

"No thanks necessary. Just make sure there are some extra dead presidents in my paycheck."

Before Miguel could say anything else, his informant disconnected the call. Normally he'd consult with his team, but time was of the essence since their possible unsub was on the move. With another call to his Seattle PD contact, he passed on the information and asked them to provide backup.

If luck was on their side, the Freedom Fascist would be in custody in no time and they'd be able to interview him. He hung up and headed out to update his team, including eating some crow that his team's top choice might actually be their unsub despite his earlier hesitation.

His people, including Liam and David, were sitting around the table, sharing a story about one of their assignments with Maisy, who sat rapt next to his empty chair. As he walked in, laughter erupted as Nicholas described his role in the capture of the unsub.

"The unsub went up and over the fence and I followed, only I didn't count on the slope on the other side of the fence. One second I was on my feet and the next I was heading down that hill," he said and gestured with his hands to show his roll. "But it was like bowling for unsubs since I knocked him off his feet as I tumbled down the hill."

"And Madeline was there to finish the collar, high heels and all," Dash teased.

"After clearing the fence and not rolling down the hill," Madeline said.

"Girl power," Maisy added.

Madeline beamed her a smile and said, "Totally."

Which was the perfect time for Miguel to step into the conversation. "You guys nailed it with your choice of unsub. I just spoke to a confidential informant who says Bob was bragging about the bombings. The CI gave me some info on where Bob might be. Seattle PD is on their way to provide backup. We need to make the collar."

The team leaped into action, rushing to get their bulletproof vests and weapons and as he went to do the same, Maisy laid a hand on the sleeve of his suit jacket. *"¡Cuídate!"*

He smiled, took hold of her hand and gave a reassuring squeeze. "I will. Liam and David will be here for anything you need."

"I just need for you to come back in one piece."

Warmth filled him with her touch and her concern. "Count on it," he said and for the first time ever, he was able to imagine the fear that his father must have felt every time his mother walked out the door. Maybe because for the first time ever, he was the one who had someone waiting for him to get home safe.

It was a humbling revelation, but he tried not to think on it too long because that would be too much of a distraction. Instead, with another squeeze of her hand, he slipped away to get ready.

THE CROWD MILLING in front of the courthouse was luckily not that big and for the most part, not that violent, unlike some earlier activities. Many of the protesters were masked in one way or another. There

was a sea of black bandannas, balaclavas and hood-
ies, but brightly colored Halloween masks broke up
the darkness of the throng. In that darkness there was
only one person in a pig mask wearing the clothing
his CI had detailed.

There were about a dozen uniformed police officers along the edges of the crowd as he and his team
arrived. Silently he directed Madeline and Nicholas
to approach their unsub from one side while he and
Dash would close the cage from the other.

They walked quickly toward the man, but as some
in the crowd noticed them, they began to be jostled
and pushed around and a murmur of warning started.
It caused their unsub to look back toward the growing commotion and as he spotted their jackets and
bulletproof vests with the bold yellow FBI mark-
ings, he bolted.

Madeline and Nicholas gave chase, driving the
unsub toward Dash and Miguel. Dash took off first
and Miguel followed more slowly, mindful of his
limitations because of his leg. But as the unsub
ducked and weaved through the crowd and the protesters made it difficult for his team, Miguel made
a direct path toward the edge of the crowd and corralled a few officers for assistance.

As the unsub neared the hoped-for freedom of
open sidewalk, with his team fighting to give chase,
Miguel and his assembled officers flanked the unsub,
cutting off his escape. The unsub stopped short at
the sight of them waiting for him, but then dodged

to one side, as if he would be able to squeeze by the small opening between one police officer and the wall of the courthouse.

The crowd, seeing what was happening, pushed toward that spot as if to open the space up for the unsub, but Miguel rushed around and blocked that last little avenue of escape. Seconds later, their unsub was wrapped in a cocoon of police officers while his team held off the few crowd members brave enough to go after them in the hopes of freeing their comrade.

At their car they wasted little time removing the unsub's mask to confirm his identity and handcuffing him while reading him his Miranda rights. Once he was bundled in the car, they raced back to the BAU offices and hauled him up to their interrogation room. For safety's sake, two FBI agents from their office and two Seattle PD officers stood guard outside the room.

As he entered the room, he caught sight of Maisy from the corner of his eye as she sat at their worktable. She offered him a smile filled with comfort and he returned it, but then all his focus was directed at the unsub as he sat down.

Madeline and he sat to conduct the interview while Nicholas and Dashiell watched from the room next door through the one-way mirror.

Madeline began, using the good-cop voice and demeanor that she had perfected in the many years they'd done this dance with other unsubs. "For the

record, this is an interrogation with Special Agent
Madeline Striker and Supervisory Special Agent
Miguel Peters interviewing Robert Smith. Bob,
you've been read your Miranda rights. Do you understand that anything you say or do can be held
against you in a court of law and that you're entitled
to counsel? If you can't afford counsel, we can provide one for you. Do you wish to continue with this
interview at this time?"

Bob negligently tossed his handcuffed hands in
the air and shrugged. "I've got nothing to hide. Mind
telling me why you're violating my civil right to protest by bringing me here?"

"I assume you're aware that there have been several bombings in the Seattle area," Madeline said.

"Who isn't? It's been all over the news," Bob said
with another, almost insolent, shrug.

"But you have more intimate knowledge of the
bombings, don't you, Bob?" Miguel said, leaning forward slightly to be in the unsub's face a little more.

Bob was unfazed. If anything, he grew more bel-
ligerent, likewise leaning forward until he was almost nose-to-nose with Miguel. "As if you guys have
something on me. You're incompetent. Stupid. That's
all over the news too."

Miguel didn't back away, determined to play hard-
ball, while Madeline said, "Bob, you know better
than that. We have someone who heard you claiming
responsibility for the bombings. Your past manifes-
tos are in line with the Seattle Crusader's demands.

We're just waiting for DNA results from the bombs and I'm sure they're going to point to you."

Bob laughed and fell back against his chair, shaking his head. "Just shows how stupid you are. Do you think *I'd* be stupid enough to leave DNA behind?"

"You were stupid enough to get caught planting a box filled with M-80s at the courthouse. You know M-80s are illegal unless you're licensed, right? Just like dynamite and I doubt you have a license," Miguel said.

"But almost any idiot can buy a gun, right?" Bob countered, a derisive smile on his face.

"I understand you did a beautiful job of wiring those M-80s. If they hadn't caught you, it would have made quite a big bang," Miguel said.

Another shrug greeted him and then Bob turned his attention to Madeline. "You'd think you would understand why we do this. Why we're trying to break the system."

Madeline didn't allow him to faze her. "Why bombs? And where did you get the dynamite?"

"Easy, Madeline. I can call you Madeline, right?" Bob said, slipping on a smarmy smile.

"Yes, of course. Please tell me. How did you get the dynamite and wire? How did you choose the kinds of bombs to build?" she said.

"Friends in the right places. As for building them, I like to tinker."

"Tinker? How do you tinker?" Miguel said, his gut telling him that something wasn't right about

Bob Smith. So not right that he was beginning to think, as he had at first, that this was not their unsub.

"I play around—"

"With dynamite. Amazing that you're still alive," Miguel shot back.

That smarmy smile returned, and Bob held his hands up and wiggled his fingers. "Magic hands."

"Please tell us how those magic hands built the collar bomb," Madeline cajoled, her voice as sweet as Vermont syrup.

"Sure," he said and with those hands, he detailed what he had done as he spoke. "I'd seen that show on Netflix about the Pizza Bomber. And you guys offer such good information on your website. Amazing stuff really. Made it real easy."

"So why didn't it go off? Why did you seem surprised when the second bomb exploded at King Street Station?" Madeline pressed.

Bob seemed a little put off by her questions, maybe even taken aback. Again, or for the first time? The CCTV footage of the bomber had not been released to the public although there had been a number of videos posted by witnesses. However, none of the witness videos had shown that moment of surprise when the second bomb went off.

"It was a bigger blast than I expected," Bob said, but Miguel could see the beads of sweat collecting on Bob's upper lip.

"But no blast from the collar bomb. Why do you think that is?" he said.

Another careless shrug was the only answer as Bob looked down at his hands.

"Magic hands fail you, Bob? Did you trip the second bomb by accident? Not build the collar bomb right?" he pressed, leaning forward again, so far across the table and in Bob's face that it was impossible for their unsub not to see him.

He reacted like Miguel had wanted. "Get out of my face, dude. That won't work on me."

"You're lying. You don't know anything about these bombings that isn't in the news," Miguel said.

"That's not true," Bob almost shouted.

"A liar. And what you were telling those people… all lies. You're just grandstanding. Trying to make a name for yourself because you're nothing," Miguel challenged.

"I am the Seattle Crusader," he shouted back.

"Tell us more, then. If you do, we can make it easier for you," Madeline said, almost cajoling.

"You guys can't do spit," Bob parried.

"Why are you wasting our time? You don't know anything. That's obvious. Are you trying to score brownie points with your masked buddies? Will taking credit for the bombings make you feel big, little man?"

Their unsub slammed his hands on the table, the sound as loud as a gunshot in the small room. "You think you can stop us, but you can't. We're winning this war and we'll use any means necessary to do that."

"Including wasting our time," Miguel said calmly and sat back, more convinced than ever that this unsub was lying.

"If that's what it takes to show how incompetent you are. To show your Gestapo tactics to silence us, but that's not going to happen. And I'm not going to cooperate anymore. I want an attorney."

"Come on, Bob. We can't help you if you don't help us," Madeline said, her tone pleading.

"I. Want. A. Lawyer," Bob said, enunciating each and every word as slowly as molasses in winter.

Miguel rose from his chair and Madeline did the same. Looking down at the unsub, he said, "Fine. Seattle PD will escort you to their station house and you can call an attorney from there. This interview is concluded."

A second later, two Seattle police officers walked into the room to guide the unsub out, but as Bob stepped into the space, he looked around.

Their whiteboard had been removed in anticipation of the interview, but Maisy was still at the table and as the unsub saw her, he peered at Miguel. With an evil glint in his eyes and a tight smile, he said, "Angel Eyes is real pretty. Are you screwing her like the government screws all of us?"

Maisy paled, but Miguel ignored the question, which only riled Bob even more. To his surprise, Bob broke free of the police officers and chest bumped him as he screamed, "Can't perform, Peters? Is that it? Can't screw her?"

The two officers grabbed him and got him under control. "Well, Bob, you just bought yourself a charge of assaulting a Federal officer and in front of several witnesses and CCTV," Miguel said and pointed to the camera in the interview room which would have captured the attack.

"Please take him away and charge him," Miguel said, and the two officers complied, hauling off a screaming Bob, who continued to curse Miguel, the other agents and the government.

As the team reconvened around the table, Miguel said, "He's not our guy."

Chapter Eleven

Maisy couldn't believe what had just happened and what followed as each of the team members nodded at Miguel's assessment.

"He didn't seem to know anything about the collar bomb," Nicholas said.

"And those 'magic hands'? There's something off about his height, the size of his hands and those of the bomber. Is there any way to get a better approximation of the hand size?" Madeline said.

Miguel concurred with a nod. "Is that possible, Dash?"

"We can try to get more info on his physical attributes. Pupil distance, et cetera," Dashiell said and stared at Nicholas, who shifted uneasily, rocking from one side to the next on his feet. Something about the quick look he shot her had her insides twisting into a knot.

"What is it, Nicholas?" Miguel asked and likewise peered at her.

"We got a call while you were interviewing the unsub," Nicholas said and once again looked her way, making her blood run cold in anticipation of what he would say.

"Spill, Nicholas," Madeline said, clearly aware of how the delay was affecting her.

"Maisy's father reached out to us. He's seen the news and is worried about Maisy. He wants to help us any way he can to catch this bomber," Nicholas said.

Despite his words, Maisy heard the "but" behind them, as did Miguel.

"What else, Nicholas?" Miguel said.

"He'll only talk to us about the bomber if Maisy is with us. He wants to talk to her tomorrow."

For a moment the world dimmed around her and her ears went deaf. She knew the team members were discussing the request because she could see their lips moving, but she couldn't hear them. Couldn't even really do anything since her body had gone numb.

But then Miguel came to her side and touched her hand. Slowly warmth and feeling returned, spreading out from the gentle pressure of his hand on hers. "Are you okay?"

Her gaze was unfocused, shimmering with incipient tears. Her chest was heavy, almost so heavy that it was hard to breathe, but somehow she dragged in a breath and said, "I'm not sure."

THERE WAS NO doubt Maisy was upset. Her face had paled to a sickly green and tears clung to her thick lashes until the first one escaped and slipped down her cheek. He cradled her jaw and swiped the tear away. "Let's get some air."

A quick nod and she was on her feet, moving away from the table and toward Miguel's office, but he thought she needed more than that.

He slipped his arm around her waist and guided her toward the elevator. At her surprised look, he said, "We both need a break. How about a coffee?"

She nodded again and eked out, "Coffee would be nice."

As the elevator arrived, they stepped on and rode down to the lobby. They did a slow stroll across the gleaming marble tiles, out onto the street and down the block to a local coffee shop. He continued to keep her close since her body still trembled and only the faintest hint of color had returned to her features. She stumbled a bit when she ordered, obviously still discomfited.

After he'd ordered and they had their coffees, he guided her toward a table against an inside wall and far enough away from the windows to offer some privacy but allow him to keep an eye out for anything untoward. The table was also close to an emergency exit in case of trouble.

Maisy wrapped shaky hands around the coffee mug and after a few sips, he asked, "Feeling better?"

"A little."

He took a sip of his own coffee and narrowed his eyes to examine her reaction as he said, "I know you've had a surprise."

Her mug hit the tabletop hard. "An understatement. But I guess nothing about my father should surprise me anymore."

"You don't have to do it. I have no doubt—"

"But you do have doubts. I haven't known you long, but even I can see you're frustrated," she said and laid her hand over his, returning the comfort he had offered earlier.

With a shrug he said, "Not so much frustrated as concerned and puzzled. Like I have a lot of pieces, but there's one missing to complete the picture."

She squeezed his hand. "You will figure it out."

He arched a brow. "But will it be quick enough?" Shaking his head, he looked away and said, "I wish I could channel my mother. I have no doubt she'd be seeing all the pieces of that puzzle."

Maisy hesitated and peered at him over the rim of her mug. She took a sip and said, "Don't sell yourself short. You will solve this."

Much like she had just done, he delayed, unsure of himself. Unsure of the request he would have to put to her as much as he might not like it. With a deep breath, he exhaled and pushed forward.

"You don't have to talk to your dad tomorrow. I won't put you through that." She'd already suffered thanks to his actions and his recent contacts which had terrorized her.

"But could it help you?" Maisy asked, her deep blue gaze locked on his, assessing his response.

Would it? he asked himself. Although his gut and

some of the evidence so far indicated that the bomber was not acting alone, could it possibly be her father directing the attacks from prison? But if he was, would the Forest Conservation Bomber attack a location where his daughter would be? Although how could he know that?

Miguel met her gaze straight on. "I won't ask you to talk to your father. I know how much he's already hurt you."

"Would it help?" she pressed, her hands clenching the mug so tightly her fingers were white from the pressure.

He reached out and covered her hands, urged her to release the mug, and he twined his fingers with hers. Despite his misgivings about not having all the pieces of the puzzle, he had faith in his team and himself.

"We will solve this."

THE WARMTH OF his calloused hands reached deep within her, offering comfort…and more. After all, he was a handsome man, but his caring and understanding were what made him truly impossible to ignore.

But she had to ignore him because she had plans for her life and Miguel wasn't a part of those plans. Much like having her father in her life again wasn't part of what she had envisioned for herself.

But she knew how troubled he was about the investigation and she was too. She'd overheard the team's concerns about their profile for the unsub and

Miguel had been open with her about his feelings. Much the way she had been open about her fears.

Despite that, she was a strong woman, and she would not let her father control her again. Or scare her again.

"Like I said before, I know you will find the bomber. But I don't want anyone else to be hurt because of something I did. Or didn't have the courage to do."

Miguel squeezed her hands and offered her a smile filled with understanding. "Nothing you do or don't do will hurt anyone, Maisy."

"I want to help. Whatever it takes, I'm ready to do it, even if it means talking to my father. I'm only going to ask one thing. I want you to go with me tomorrow to see him."

DASHIELL PEERED AT Madeline, Nicholas, David and Liam as they gathered around the table.

"I'm not sure Maisy will go along with speaking to her father. She seemed very upset," he said.

"Not unexpected. As Nicholas mentioned, she and her mother are probably suffering from a form of PTSD so anything connected with her father is bound to cause great distress," Madeline said.

"Definitely," Nicholas chimed in. "Still, I think we all agree there may be more than one person behind this terrorism. Maybe even the Forest Conservation Bomber."

"What about Bob Smith? Is he off our lists of unsubs?" David asked.

"We did the analysis you asked on body parts, comparing the unsub's height, width, hands to the photos and videos we have, and he doesn't fit," Liam said.

Dashiell walked to the whiteboard, picked up the eraser and held it over the Freedom Fascist's name on the board. When Madeline and Nicholas nodded, he erased his name.

"Where does that leave us? Liam? David? Do you have anything else for us?" Dashiell asked.

David nodded and handed a report to everyone at the table. "We ran the photo we created against several databases and this is a list of possible suspects, complete with their pictures."

The phone in the middle of the conference table rang, rattling against the wood. Madeline reached over and hit the speakerphone button. "Yes, Lorelai. Madeline here. What can we do for you?"

"Director Branson just called. The TEDAC director called her to say they had an initial report they'd be sending to her. We should have it in less than half an hour," Lorelai said.

"Any idea what they've found?" Liam asked his ex.

"From what the director said, they've identified the dynamite and wire makers, have a couple of fingerprints and DNA. They'll be sending the profile over so you can run it through CODIS and the genealogy services."

"Great. That's wonderful, Lorelai. As soon as you have it, please send it over," Madeline said just as Miguel and Maisy walked down the hall.

Miguel immediately read their mood. "I guess we have good news?"

Dashiell nodded and said, "TEDAC report is on the way with lots of information."

"Good to hear," Miguel said and shot a half glance at Maisy. "We have news as well."

Holding his breath, Dashiell waited for what their witness—and a woman Miguel obviously cared about—would say. While he waited, he corralled his concern about how Miguel's attraction to Maisy might affect the investigation. He also once again inspected the team members gathered around the table to see how they would react to Maisy's news.

"Maisy?" Miguel prompted.

Maisy risked a glance at Miguel and after looked toward them. "Miguel and I discussed it and…I will meet with my father, but I've asked Miguel to be there."

Nicholas nodded and said, "I don't think that will be an issue. His one request was to speak to Maisy, and he has to expect that the FBI will be there as well."

Miguel clapped his hands and said, "Great. Make the call. As soon as we have the TEDAC report, let's jump on running anything they have for us. In the meantime, what else do we have?"

MAISY SAT IN a chair and watched as Miguel assumed control of the meeting. Easygoing control, she noticed again. He waited and digested what his team had gathered. Prompted their ideas and then offered his own, leading the investigation in his laid-back way. But despite that, there was no doubt who was in charge.

Power radiated from him, drawing her in while at the same time, she couldn't miss his concern that so far, they were missing key pieces of the puzzle.

The phone rang barely half an hour later, signaling that the TEDAC report had arrived. The team immediately reviewed the results together and divided up what to do with the report.

"Liam, David and I will work on running the DNA and fingerprints against the databases," Dashiell advised.

Madeline held up the list of possible suspects. "I'll do a deeper review of this list."

"I'll make arrangements for a visit tomorrow to Maisy's dad," Nicholas said.

"Good. Please forward me the TEDAC report, your lists and anything else you dig up. If Maisy doesn't mind, we'll visit my father and go over what he remembers about the bombing," Miguel stated.

Maisy dipped her head and said, "I don't mind at all. You know I love your dad."

Miguel smiled. "Thank you. Please excuse me while I step aside to call ahead and let him know we're coming."

He waited a beat for any feedback, then headed out, leaving Maisy sitting with the team. She normally wasn't comfortable about strangers, a side effect of having virtually been in hiding for the past fifteen years. Not to mention the fear still roiling her gut about seeing her father once again. But the team had made her feel comfortable and she knew they were working hard at keeping her and others safe from the Seattle Crusader.

"I want to thank you for all that you're doing," Maisy said, her comment heartfelt.

Madeline nodded and offered her a brilliant smile. "We couldn't do anything else."

A few minutes later, Miguel walked back in and laid a hand on her shoulder. "Ready?"

"Yes, thanks," she said, rose and walked beside Miguel down the hall to the elevator lobby. While they waited, Miguel glanced at her, eyes narrowed, a worried look on his features.

"Are you really ready?"

Maisy didn't know if she'd ever be "really ready" for what might happen tomorrow. She hadn't ever contemplated seeing her father again. If anything, she'd hoped she'd never have to see him again, but the Seattle Crusader had made that impossible. Regardless, she was strong enough to handle this, especially with Miguel and his team at her side.

"I'm as ready as I'll ever be."

With a slow nod, he said, "I know you will be."

The ding of the elevator shattered the moment.

Together they boarded the elevator and as they'd done earlier, traveled through the lobby and down the few blocks to the hotel where Miguel's dad was living. As he'd done earlier, he wrapped an arm around her waist and drew her close, the action one of comfort and protection. But as had happened before, it was impossible to ignore that he was a vital and attractive man.

Every now and then she'd peer up at him, take in the strong line of his jaw, slightly shaded with the start of an evening beard. Full lips, more relaxed now than in the office.

He did a quick glance down at her and their gazes locked, his brown eyes sharp, but warm as he perused her features. He smiled and a dimple emerged at the right side of his mouth, making him look more boyish. Less formidable.

But then suddenly Miguel was searching the area, back in FBI mode. She tracked his gaze, looking around, but saw nothing.

"Everything okay?" she asked.

"Just thought I saw something, but I must have imagined it," he said, gently squeezed her waist, and they continued their walk in peace.

THE SEATTLE CRUSADER CURSED and clung to the trunk of the tree he'd hidden behind. Counting to ten, he sucked in a deep breath and peeked past the trunk.

Seeing Angel Eyes and the FBI agent walking away, he blew out a relieved exhale and did another count of ten before following them again.

If it was up to him, he'd be back home in the tent he'd set up in the homeless encampment under the highway and smoking some weed. But he had his instructions and if he was going to help his brothers, not to mention himself, he had to do as he was told.

That meant finding out where the two witnesses were being held, as well as the location of the BAU office. The latter was easy enough. He'd only had to search the web to get the address of the building.

But learning where the witnesses were had been harder. It had forced him to surveil the FBI offices since yesterday in addition to planting the two bombs last night.

He laughed as he thought of how well those bombings had gone off and the attention that his tweets had gotten. It was going just as planned, which reminded him that he had another tweet to share tonight.

Yanking out the burner phone he'd been provided, he stopped and tweeted.

Time for criminal reform. No bail. Shorter jail terms. Fairer parole policies. It's time to decriminalize before it's too late.

His phone made a little whoosh sound as he touched Send and the tweet hit the outside world.

But as he looked up, he realized that he had lost sight of Angel Eyes and the FBI agent.

Luckily, he knew they'd be returning to the FBI offices at some point.

Unluckily for them, he'd be waiting for them and would be ready to act.

Smiling, he reached into his pocket and took out the cash he'd been paid. More than enough for a nice dinner tonight. And once he finished his tasks, he'd have enough for daily meals and a place to stay. A place big enough for him and his brothers once they were released, as he'd been promised.

With a whistle, he shoved the money back into his pocket, turned and headed for his favorite pub, dreaming of the biggest burger they made.

The first of many, he thought. Just a few more tweets and bombs, and he'd be set for life.

Chapter Twelve

This is what a family should be like, Maisy thought as she sat at the small hotel table with Miguel and his dad.

They'd been chatting amiably about Maisy's blog, but also about her suggestion that his father, Robert, help other budding bloggers and journalists with the knowledge he'd gleaned over the years as a professor. Sadly, the discussion soon turned to the investigation and how Maisy was supposed to speak to her father in the morning as well as trying to glean what they could about what Robert remembered from the day of the bombing. Unfortunately his father remembered very little.

"It's okay, Dad," Miguel said, but his general frustration about the investigation was painfully obvious.

"I know I'm missing something, Dad. And I know that if *Mami* was alive she'd see what I'm missing," Miguel said.

Robert reached out and laid his hand on Miguel's shoulder. "Trust in yourself. You are your mother's son, but more importantly, you are brilliant in your own special way."

A half smile relieved Miguel's too serious features, making him look younger. "Thanks, Dad."

"I agree, Robert. Miguel and his team are making progress. I have no doubt they'll catch the Seattle Crusader in no time."

Much like Robert had done before, he reached out and laid a comforting hand on her shoulder. Funny thing, she had thought Miguel's touchiness had come from his Cuban mother, but Robert was also as demonstrative.

"I understand you have to face your own challenge, Maisy. Am I right?"

With a sideways glance at Miguel, Maisy said, "I have to see my father tomorrow."

A little hum escaped Robert before he said, "And how does that make you feel?"

She inhaled a breath, trapped it inside her. Slowly she let it escape and said, "Scared—no, make that terrified. What he did and after, it terrorized my mom and me for so long. I never wanted to see him again and now…" Her voice trailed off, her throat choked with emotion. Tears were once again threatening, making her sniffle as she battled them.

"It's okay to be scared. Terrified," Miguel said and covered her hand with his.

Comfort filled her as it did so often with his touch. Peace, something which had been sorely lacking in her life during the past fifteen years.

"But you'll be there, right? To help me?" she said, not sure she could face her father without his support.

"I'll be there. Always," he said and as her gaze locked with his, it was too easy to imagine an always with him.

"Thank you," she said.

The chirp of Miguel's phone shattered the moment. "Please excuse me," he said, rose from the table and walked a few feet away to take the call in more privacy. Still, the room was small, making it impossible not to eavesdrop.

"Okay. 9:00 a.m. tomorrow. Sea Tac. We'll meet you in the lobby at eight fifteen."

He ended the call and from across the short distance, his gaze met hers as if seeking her confirmation.

With a nod, she said, "I'll be ready."

She says it, but is she really ready? Miguel wondered. He didn't know if he would be, recalling how he'd suffered after his mother's murder and how it still affected him at times. How it hung over him, keeping him from moving on, he realized with surprise.

Much like Maisy had been a prisoner of her past, so had he and maybe it was time to change that.

"We should get going. We have an early morning."

He walked back to the table. Maisy and his father had risen, and he took a moment to hug his father. Hard. "Goodnight, Dad."

Maisy drifted over to likewise embrace his father. "Thank you for everything, Robert. Miguel is so very lucky to have you."

"And now you have me too. I'm here for you."

Maisy smiled, an enchanting smile. Her gaze glittered joyfully, devoid of the pain that had clouded her beautiful blue eyes earlier.

The sight of her, so much happier, lightened the pain and anxiety in his heart, prompting him to take her into his arms. "You're not alone anymore."

She hugged him, her head tucked against his chest. Her slender arms wrapped around him. "I know."

They ended the embrace, and his father offered his routine but heartfelt send-off. *"¡Cuídate!"*

Miguel smiled and said, "Love you."

After his father opened the door so they could leave, he kept his arm around Maisy's waist as they walked out of the hotel room, bid goodnight to the FBI agent stationed at the door and strolled the few short blocks back to the BAU offices.

Back to my home, only it isn't much of a home, is it? he thought.

But as Maisy and he stepped into his apartment, it felt different. It felt not as…lonely.

He stopped and faced her. Cradled her cheek and applied gentle pressure to tilt her face upward. "It's my turn to thank you," he said.

She narrowed her gaze and skipped it over his features, puzzled. "Why?"

"Because you've helped me more than you can

imagine," he said and stroked his thumb across the creamy skin of her cheek.

Her lips quirked up in a smile and she shook her head. "That's hard to believe."

"Believe it. Your strength in dealing with your past… It's made me think about my past. My mom. That pain I still carry with me every day."

She smoothed a hand across his chest and then laid it over his heart. "But we have to find a way to put it away, don't we? It's the only way we can build a future."

A future? he thought. Suddenly he wasn't as closed off to a future that was about more than just work. *A future that includes this amazing woman,* he thought and bent his head, covered her half smile with his lips.

Her lips were warm against his. So soft and mobile as she returned his kiss, rising on tiptoes to meet him more fully. Pressing her lush body to his, her curves flattening against him, rousing passion.

He tightened his hold on her, relishing the feel of her. The way the warmth of her body seeped into his, kindling heat within him. But not just the heat of passion. Kindling fire and life in his heart.

As the kiss deepened, so did the need to touch her. He inched his hand between them to cup her breast, and her nipple beaded beneath his palm. She moaned and he hesitated, but then she covered his hand with hers, urging him on.

He tugged at the hard nub, dragging another moan

from her. The moan ripped through the haze of passion, jerking him back to the reality of their situation.

It must have done the same for her as in unison, they uneasily eased apart, gazes locked. Arms still wrapped around one another.

"I'm sorry. I shouldn't have done that," he said, but took no other motion to break apart from her.

"Don't apologize. I'm as responsible," she replied and reached up to wipe her thumb across his lips. The touch sent another zing of need through him, but she offered him a wry smile and said, "Lip gloss."

He chuckled and nodded. "Not quite what the other agents expect me to be wearing."

"No, but it looks good on you," she said and as her gaze settled on his face again, it was hot. Possessive.

"But it looks way better on you." He couldn't resist slipping his thumb across her mouth, the touch possibly more intimate than their kiss.

His phone chirped and he reached between their bodies to pull it out, glance at the face of it and swipe to take the call. "Dashiell. Do you have something new?"

"Another tweet from the Crusader. This one calls for no bail and shorter prison terms for drug possession. Another threat that a bomb is on its way unless we do as he asks."

"I'll check it out. In the meantime, ask Madeline to see if anyone on that list or a relative has been jailed."

"On it. We'll keep you posted if anything else hits tonight."

Dashiell ended the call and Miguel finally took the step back from Maisy. He had to refocus his attention on the case to keep her and others safe.

"I need to review the new information," he said, and Maisy nodded.

Maisy gestured toward the bathroom. "I think I'll take a shower and get ready for bed."

"Great. I'm going to see what we have so far and shower in the morning," he said.

"Great," she parroted, obviously growing uneasier by the second despite their earlier closeness.

"Great," he said and wanted to kick himself for how stupid it sounded. Luckily, she bolted to her bag to grab some clothes and then to the shower.

He blew out a harsh breath and dragged a hand through his hair in frustration. He was used to cases not going the way he wanted, but this case was getting way too complicated.

First there was the bomber himself and their inability to stop him. He seemed to have no interest in harming anyone yet, but for how long? Eventually he would escalate the situation and possibly hurt someone.

The sound of flowing water in the shower intruded and reminded him that it was best he get ready for bed before Maisy emerged from the bathroom, shower fresh. Skin flushed from the hot water.

He muttered a curse as passion rose again and he leaped into action.

Quickly changing into sweats and a T-shirt, which would let him rush up to the office in case he needed to, he tugged down the Murphy bed and settled there with his laptop.

He pulled up his notes and, in his brain, worked through the bomber's assorted requests, which were starting to add to his profile of the typical serial bomber.

White male. In it for either revenge or justification. The demands were continuing to be unrealistic, but he ran through them anyway.

A higher minimum wage. *Maybe someone stuck in assorted low-paying jobs?*

The homeless encampment in the Japanese Gardens. *Possibly someone who has experienced homelessness?*

The demand for bail and prison reform added a dimension that actually narrowed the list of possible suspects to someone directly touched by that system. It was why he'd asked his people to see if anyone on their list had relatives in prison.

Which directed his thoughts toward Maisy's father. He had tossed around the idea in his brain of the Forest Conservation Bomber being involved with the bombings, but the motivations were too disparate. Protecting the environment versus the assorted social issues raised by the Crusader.

The methods of the bombings were also too different. Fertilizer-based bombs versus ones made with dynamite.

Finally, Maisy's dad had intended to do harm. *Had* done harm and so far, the Crusader's targets were clearly in areas where no one would be hurt, especially since the detonator on the collar bomb had not been connected.

"So far" being the operative words, which propelled him to continue working, trying to get closer to the persons behind the bombings. He was sure of that one thing: the bomber wasn't acting alone. There was language in the demands that pointed to that and his gut told him the bomber was a puppet and someone else was pulling the strings.

Maybe even Rothwell. There was something about the politician and his too-convenient appearance whenever something happened that bothered him. And it had nothing to do with the politician's insults.

He'd been insulted before and by better than Richard Rothwell.

Armed with that thought, he pushed on, determined to have more to the Crusader's profile by the time they met with Maisy's dad in the morning.

MAISY LINGERED IN the shower even though she knew that no matter how long she took, Miguel would be awake and working hard on catching the bomber.

A bomber just like my dad, she thought as she shut off the water and toweled down.

A bomber who she feared would one day hurt or kill someone just like her father had done.

No, not my father, she reminded herself. As she'd told Miguel, her father had died the day that the Forest Conservation Bomber had been born.

She had died that day as well. Elizabeth Green, the young girl who had dreamed of traveling and writing, had disappeared and been replaced by Maisy Oliver, a woman who had been afraid and in hiding for the past fifteen years.

But she'd made her mother and herself a promise as she'd watched her mother slowly die from cancer: that she'd start to live again. That she'd dream again, the dreams she'd had as a child.

She was not going to let this bomber, or her dad, defeat her.

Slipping into her pajamas, she tiptoed from the bathroom to not distract Miguel, but as she caught sight of him, she suspected his attention was totally focused on his work.

Until he spotted her, and slowly lifted his gaze. "Good night, Maisy."

"Good night, Miguel."

Even though it had grown late what with their visiting his dad, the dinner they'd picked up and shared after that visit, and a pleasantly long hot shower, she was too wired to sleep.

She made up the couch with the sheets, comforter and pillow, and settled in, making sure that she was nestled deep in the comfortable cushions and unable to see Miguel because he was way too distracting.

She grabbed her tablet, plugged in earphones and went to a streaming service to try to catch up on a series that she had been watching about unique buildings. It wasn't just the architecture that captured her interest, but the equally fascinating settings for many of the structures.

She had pictured herself visiting such different locales and writing about them. It was why she'd worked so hard after her mom had died to find a better-paying job. A job she had unfortunately had to put on hold with this investigation. Luckily, her new boss understood why she was absent, but she was eager to go back to work. Back to her normal life and her dreams.

And nothing, not her father, this bomber or even Miguel, was going to keep her from that.

Chapter Thirteen

The Forest Conservation bomber was being held at the federal detention center, a multipurpose prison that held various types of detainees. It wasn't far from the airport so the ride to get there wasn't that long. Unbeknownst to Maisy and her mother, their flight from their Woodinville hometown to escape her father's crimes had actually put them closer to where he was being imprisoned.

And although the ride wasn't long, it was silent and tense.

Miguel sat beside Maisy in the back seat while Nicholas drove, with Madeline in the passenger seat.

Maisy was pale and as Miguel laid his hand on hers, her skin was ice-cold even with the heat in the car.

"It'll be fine," Miguel urged, trying to calm her.

She nodded and forced a smile, but her distress was plain to see. Her amazing blue eyes were dead, almost cold. Every muscle in her body tense except for a nervous tic at her jaw.

He twined his fingers with hers, trying to offer

what comfort he could through the rest of the drive and the process for being cleared for entry into the detention center.

As this was a special visit, the warden met them as soon as they went through security and walked them to a room normally used for visits by attorneys. "I hope you get what you want from Green. He's a tough nut," the warden said.

"Has he given you problems?" Miguel asked the older man.

With a shrug, the warden said, "He's not violent despite his criminal record. Just a know-it-all, trying to challenge every rule or regulation. He thinks he's smarter than everyone."

Which just confirms part of our profile, Miguel thought. Serial bombers, much like serial killers, thought they were more intelligent than everyone around them.

"We appreciate that heads-up as well as allowing this visit on such short notice," Miguel said and shook the other man's hand.

"Not a problem, SSA Peters. We understand the urgency of the situation. Whenever you're ready," the older man said and gestured toward the door to the visiting room.

Miguel peered at Maisy. "Are you ready?"

HER THROAT WAS so tight, her heart pounding hard enough to split her chest open, that Maisy couldn't speak. She could only nod and brace herself for her first look at her father in fifteen years.

As she walked in, she thought, *He's aged.*

His once caramel brown hair had gone gray and the lines around his mouth and eyes had deepened. Despite that, his skin was tanned and his body whip-cord lean, as if he'd been exercising. It almost wasn't fair that he looked that good when she thought about how her mother had suffered and deteriorated thanks to the cancer that had claimed her life.

"Elizabeth. Or should I call you Maisy now?" Richard Green said and before she could reply, he added, "You've grown into such a lovely young woman. You look so much like your mother."

"Mr. Green. Supervisory Special Agent Peters," Miguel said and then gestured to his team members. "Special Agent Striker and Special Agent James are also attending this interview."

At his words, her father almost seemed to preen, as if having that many FBI agents was testament to his importance. "Thank you for coming, especially you, Maisy. I hope you understand that I never meant to hurt you and your mother. And I never meant to hurt anyone. I was just trying to defend something that couldn't defend itself."

Which was what he'd said throughout his trial although the investigators had provided numerous proofs of his intent to maim and kill loggers and other people the Forest Conservation League had seen as enemies. Clearly her father still didn't believe he deserved to be in jail for what he'd done.

"But you did hurt and kill," she shot back, not buying his apology.

Her father's face hardened, growing tense. "I had hoped you could forgive me. That's why I've been trying to reach you. The calls and letters were my way of trying to make peace with you because even though I'm in prison, I'm still your father. And I love you, Maisy. You have to believe that."

Miguel laid a hand on her shoulder and applied gentle pressure, urging her to sit across from her father.

She hated to do it, almost felt like it was accepting his apology, something she wasn't prepared to do. But she knew she had to keep the lines of communication open to hopefully get some useful information for the Seattle Crusader investigation. But there was something she needed to know first.

"How did you find out my new name and address?" she asked.

Her father smiled, but it held no warmth or happiness. "I have my ways, Maisy. Friends who still appreciate what I did and help me."

It made her wonder if those friends were behind what was happening, and Miguel must have felt the same way.

"I guess that means you may have insights for us," Miguel said.

Her father nodded and skipped his gaze over

the stern faces of the three FBI agents. "I do. This bomber is a novice. He doesn't know what he's doing, almost like he's shooting off big M-80s to get attention."

"Why do you say that?" Maisy asked, taking the lead.

"If I had made the bomb, it would have taken out more of the buildings and the old man in the station. This bomber doesn't really know how to use dynamite to its full potential."

"You mean how to hurt someone, don't you? Like the people you hurt. Like you hurt Mom and me. Do you even care that you did that?" she shot back, unable to stay silent.

Her father reached for her hand, but she pulled it back, dreading his touch.

With a shake of his head and a harsh laugh, he said, "You're so cold, just like your mother. But despite that, I did care for her and you. I still care. That's why I asked you to visit. I want to help."

"If you want to help, tell us what else you know," Nicholas said, jumping into the conversation.

"Like I said, he's a novice, not like me. He doesn't understand the power he has and how to use it. If he did, he would make reasonable demands," her father said.

"Like asking for money like you did?" Maisy countered.

Her father glared at her. "Money that I intended

to use to buy wilderness areas in danger of being destroyed."

"Do you think he's working alone?" Miguel asked.

Her father's answer was immediate. "No, I don't. Someone is directing him because he's a novice. Stupid almost. Someone much more intelligent is pulling the puppet's strings," he said and mimicked someone playing a marionette.

"Someone like you?" Madeline asked, arching a dark brow in emphasis.

"Me? You think I'm involved?" her father said, clearly incredulous at the question.

"Do you even care that he's targeting me, Dad? Angel Eyes? Does that matter to you?" Maisy pressed.

"Of course it does. Why do you think you're here?" he said, his gaze almost pleading as it traveled across her face and then over the FBI agents.

Miguel answered, "I think we're here to satisfy your ego. Your need to be better than the Crusader. To prove how much smarter you are than him and us. That's why I think we're here because so far, you haven't told us a thing we don't know."

"I *am* better than the Crusader. And to tell you something you don't know, he's going to strike again and this time, he's going to hurt someone," her father parried.

Maisy risked a glance at Miguel, and it was obvious that he was done, especially considering that nothing her father had said, not even his last outburst, had provided any useful information.

Pushing to her feet, she said, "I'd like to go, but before I do." She faced her father. "Do not contact me again, *Richard*. You're not my father. The father I had was kind and gentle and not a monster like you."

WHEN RICHARD GREEN lunged at Maisy, Miguel blocked his arm and pushed him back into his seat. "You heard the lady. I'm going to make sure the warden knows of your harassment and blocks your mail and phone access."

"You can't do that!" Richard shouted, but Maisy was already in motion, rushing toward the door, flanked by Madeline and Nicholas. Miguel followed, tuning out the Forest Conservation Bomber's shouts that chased them as they exited.

When his team members shifted to walk in front of Maisy for protection, Miguel slipped to her side and wrapped an arm around her waist. She was trembling, but her head was held high. "You are amazing," he whispered in her ear.

"I'm my mother's daughter," she replied, meeting his eyes, her cerulean gaze direct and blazing with anger and determination.

"She must have been an incredible woman," he said and hugged her close, but that action drew raised eyebrows from both Madeline and Nicholas.

Despite that, he didn't pull away from Maisy, walking with his arm around her until they were out of the detention center and at their car. Once they were settled in the back seat, he said, "I appreciate you doing this. I know how hard it must have been for you to see your father."

Maisy shook her head. "Like I told him, he's not my father. My father is dead."

Miguel nodded. "I understand. I just wish that we would have gotten some useful information, given the pain you suffered by coming here."

Madeline twisted slightly in the passenger seat to look back at them. "In a way we did. Green confirmed much of our profile."

"You're right about that, Madeline. He has confirmed our profile, but that also has me worrying about when the Crusader will strike again and who he might harm," Nicholas said with a quick glance at them as he drove.

"Which means we need to keep on pushing to get more info. Hopefully Dash's team has more info on the list of licensed blasters as well as the DNA profile." Miguel whipped out his smartphone to call the team back at the BAU offices.

Dashiell answered, an upbeat tone in his voice. "Good morning."

"From the sound of your voice I guess it is a good morning," Miguel said and fixed his gaze on Maisy's face while he listened to Dash's report. Her eyes locked with his, expectant.

"We have a list of blasters and we've been able

to limit it to those who have access to the type of dynamite used."

"How many blasters do we have to chase down?" he asked.

"Six, and at least two of them are working at sites owned by guess who," Dash said, excitement filtering into his tone.

"Let me guess. Rothwell," Miguel responded, pleased that his gut instinct was possibly not too far off.

"Bingo. Rothwell. Plus, we've also refined the list we gave Madeline to focus on anyone with family members who might have criminal backgrounds. Unfortunately, that list is still fairly long," Dash said, some of the enthusiasm leaving his voice.

"That's still progress. What about the DNA profile?" he pressed.

A heavy sigh filtered across the line. "No match in CODIS. Whoever he is, he's managed not to be in trouble with the law."

"A novice much like our profile said," Miguel said and shifted his gaze to meet Madeline's and Nicholas's for the barest moment.

"I'm just the tech guy, but if I had to guess, the Crusader hasn't been at this long and is probably being directed by someone else," Dash said, and in the background, someone called out to him, clearly needing his attention.

"I have to go."

Miguel peered out the window to see where they were. "We'll be there in about five minutes."

Five minutes to jump back into the investigation, but that also meant they might be running off to speak to the blasters and the most promising leads on their list of suspects identified by their facial recognition software. Which would leave Maisy sitting by herself in either their offices or his apartment for long hours.

"We may need to leave you alone to continue with the investigation," he said.

"I'll be fine. Don't worry about me. Maybe I could even go visit your father," she said and patted his hand.

But he did worry about her, cared about her, maybe more than he should. And even though it would be nice for her to visit his father, and his father would likely appreciate the company, it was an iffy thing. "I may not be able to protect you if you go to visit him."

"I understand you have other responsibilities, and I don't want to be a bother," she said, but he could see she was a little disappointed. A visit to his dad would let her work on her travel blog and it would do his father good as well.

Despite his better judgment, he found himself saying, "I could have another agent take you over and back if that's okay with you."

Her smile was the only answer he needed.

Chapter Fourteen

Maisy loved spending time with Miguel's dad. He was so kind and caring and in love with sharing his knowledge. But she also loved sharing what she knew, and they spent the better part of the afternoon making a website for Robert so that he could post articles about writing and journalism. They also set up a way for people to contact him in case they wished for him to do a speaking engagement.

"Thank you so much for helping me with that," Robert said and sat back, a broad smile on his face.

"It was my pleasure. You've given me so much useful information," Maisy said and hit a button to save the contact page on the site.

"Together we are formidable pair," Robert declared with a laugh, but his mood dimmed quickly, and Maisy understood why.

"We will stay in touch. I promise," she said.

"I know, my dear. It's just that…you'd be so good for Miguel. He needs someone like you in his life," Robert said, but then busied himself with gathering the papers where he'd been jotting down notes on using the website and ideas for articles and work-shops.

"Your son and me… It's complicated," she said, snapped her laptop shut and slipped it into her knap-sack.

"I may be old, but I understand what that means. It was complicated for my Gloria and me, but we found a way to be together. To have a happy life until… It was worth the pain," Robert said and snif-fled as he pulled off his glasses, closed his eyes and pressed his fingers at the bridge of his nose to hold back his tears.

Maisy rose from her chair and embraced Robert, held him tight until he sucked in a rough breath and said, "I'm fine, my dear. Just fine."

Maisy was sure he would be because he had peo-ple in his life who cared about him—his son for start-ers. She'd seen how Miguel treated his dad, no matter how exasperated his father made him.

Robert was a lucky man to have people who cared.

She had no one.

You have Miguel, the little voice in her head said, but Maisy wagged her head to shake loose that thought.

A knock came at the door and at Robert's "Come in," the FBI agent who had escorted her over walked into the room.

"Sorry to interrupt, but we should be heading back," the agent suggested.

"Not a problem. We just finished," Maisy said, slipped on her jacket and grabbed her knapsack.

She returned to Robert's side, hugged him hard and said, "I'll come back again soon."

Robert returned the embrace and said, "Take care."

She smiled and nodded. "I will."

The agent and she exited Robert's hotel room and made the return trip to the BAU offices, the agent alert to what was happening around them. He constantly scanned the area and stayed close to her, making her feel both safe and worried at the same time. Despite the Seattle Crusader's threat to harm someone and his mention of her, Maisy didn't think he'd actually go through with it.

But as they reached the building housing the BAU offices, a blur of black and gray snagged her attention and also that of the agent. He shoved her behind him and turned in the direction of the motion and as she peered past his arm, she saw the man with the ski mask standing less than twenty feet away. He wore the same hoodie and jeans as the Seattle Crusader.

The FBI agent held his hand up, whipped out his pistol, and said, "FBI. Put your hands up!"

At that the man turned and started to run. The agent was about to give chase when the world exploded beside them. The force of the blast knocked them down and bits and pieces of glass and concrete rained down on them. After the noise of the explosion faded, the blare of car alarms from nearby automobiles sounded, triggered by the force of the blast.

Maisy's ears were ringing, and her elbow ached from where she had been thrown to the ground by the force of the blast. She examined her injury and noticed that her jacket was torn, her elbow skinned and bleeding.

She started to stand, but the FBI agent with her laid a gentle hand on her shoulder and said, "Hold on, miss. Let's get that bleeding stopped."

She wanted to say it was just a skinned elbow, but then she tracked his gaze to her other arm. A sharp tear ran across her jacket and blood flowed freely from beneath it. The agent helped her ease the jacket sleeve off to reveal the gash across her upper arm. Then he quickly whipped off his tie and wrapped it around the wound, making it tight enough to stop the bleeding.

He had barely finished when Miguel rushed up to them, followed by Madeline and Nicholas. He knelt by her and placed an arm across her back to offer support.

"How bad?" he asked the agent who had been guarding her.

"Not too deep, I think. I haven't had a chance to check out anything else," the agent explained.

"We'll get on it," Madeline said and quickly directed Nicholas, the agent guarding her and the other agents who'd streamed out of the building to safeguard the area and any evidence.

The blast had taken out part of a pillar on the building housing the BAU offices and the force of the blast had shattered all the glass along the one side of the building as well as a few stories above the pillar.

The sound of an ambulance pulling up drew Miguel's attention. "Let's get you over to the EMT," he said and helped her to her feet. Her knees were wobbly, and she needed his support to walk over to the ambulance. But seconds later she was seated in the ambulance and an EMT was working on her arm.

"Not very deep. She won't need stitches," he said as he tenderly cleaned the wound.

She winced at the bite of the antiseptic and he apologized. "Sorry."

"No worries," she answered, but at Miguel's muttered curse, she met his worried gaze. "I'm okay. Really," she said to reassure him.

"You could have been killed," he said and dragged a hand through his hair in frustration.

"I'm okay, but the Crusader was here. We saw him right before the blast."

I SHOULD HAVE been here, Miguel thought, concern for her overriding all his thoughts.

This is what it's like to care for someone. To think of nothing but them even when the world around you is on fire, he thought.

But he didn't have the luxury of that in his life. He couldn't care for someone as deeply as he cared for Maisy because his focus had to be on the bigger picture. On his responsibilities for others.

"We'll find him. Right now, I need to get you

safely inside the BAU office, but I have to oversee my team. Are you up for it?" he asked as he glanced at the EMT, who signaled he was done with Maisy.

"I am. You go. I know you have responsibilities."

He was about to respond when Dashiell raced over, Liam and David tagging behind him, which was perfect.

"Dashiell, I need you to take Maisy back up to the office and get her interview while her memories are fresh. She also indicated that they'd seen the Crusader right before the blast, so please check CCTV cameras and find out what you can."

"Got it, Miguel," Dashiell said and held his hand out to Maisy. She slipped her hand into his and Miguel's gut tightened.

With jealousy? Over Dash, who had no interest in her, especially since he'd found his own special someone just a short time ago? Miguel thought and once again had to tell himself to focus on what was important at the moment, namely finding the bomber who was terrorizing Seattle.

"I'll be up as soon as I can," he said and ran his hand down her back in a gesture meant to reassure.

"I know you will," she said with such trust, his heart constricted.

He'd already failed her, but he wouldn't do it again. As they headed toward the door to the BAU's office building, he marched over to the side of the structure where the explosion had taken out part of one of the support pillars for the building. Luckily, it seemed like minor damage at the blast site. An ATF agent and Mack from Seattle ABS were already there, examining the pillar. Police tape had already been set up around the perimeter of their crime scene, and he eased under it and headed toward the men, mindful of not stepping on any possible evidence.

Like before, he noticed bits of paper and hints of blue wire. At the blast site, Mack and the ATF agent were examining the damage.

As he approached, Mack rose, shook his hand and introduced the ATF agent. "Special Agent Cummings."

"SSA Peters. Good to work with you. What have we got?" he asked the two bomb experts.

"Dynamite again. Enough to make a substantial blast, but not do major damage," ATF Agent Cummings said.

"The blast created a lot of shrapnel from the glass of the building and the concrete of the pillar, but it's surface damage," Mack added in explanation.

"Maybe because he was here and didn't want to get hurt himself," Miguel said.

"The Crusader was here? In the area?" Mack asked and searched the surrounding area, not that the Crusader would be stupid enough to hang around.

"Maisy said she and the agent guarding her saw him right before the blast. I have Dash and his team checking out the CCTV footage to see what we have."

"Keep us posted," Special Agent Cummings said and sank back down onto his haunches to review the blast site again.

With a nod, Miguel left the two men to their investigation and headed upstairs, eager to hear what his team might have found and to see Maisy and make sure she was okay.

Maisy, Maisy, Maisy. She'd been on his brain the entire morning as they'd run down their prospective leads, speaking to two of the licensed blasters. Neither had raised alarms with him and they still had another four to go, but that would have to wait now while they processed any new evidence from this blast.

It was another explosion that would have likely not injured anyone, although there were never any guarantees. People could have heart attacks from the shock, like in the Olympic Park Bomber case. The shrapnel that had cut Maisy's arm could have easily slashed her neck and a vital artery.

His heart sunk to somewhere in the middle of his gut as he imagined Maisy gone from his life. Taken by a terrorist the way his mother had been, way too soon.

Way, way too soon because he hadn't really had a chance to get to know her.

Which is how it has to stay, he reminded himself.

Rushing into the building, he hurried to the elevator, hands jammed into his pants pockets, feet tapping as he waited for it to arrive. As the ding announced the elevator had arrived, he barely contained himself to allow the sole passenger to exit and marched on, impatient to reach the BAU offices.

As soon as the door opened on the floor, he dashed out and into their offices. A quick look confirmed that Dashiell had likely taken Maisy to the interrogation room and he pushed on to that space. Inside, his team was sitting with Maisy as she told them what she had seen before the blast.

All heads turned in his direction as he entered. He forced a smile and went straight to Maisy's side, passing a hand across her back to offer support.

"How's it going?" he asked.

Maisy glanced up at him and said, "The bomber was there with us when the bomb went off."

He nodded. "How close was he?"

"Maybe twenty feet away. By the edges of the park next to the building," she said.

He faced Dash. "Would our cameras capture that area?"

Dash shook his head. "Probably not, but we might have caught him when he placed the bomb by the pillar. I have Liam and David reviewing the CCTV tapes to confirm that."

He nodded. "Good. Mack and ATF Special Agent Cummings will send what they have, but after an initial examination, it looks like our man again. Dynamite and blue wires. The bomb was placed and constructed in a way to make a statement."

"But possibly not hurt anyone again?" Nicholas said.

Anger surged through him. "Maisy and our agent were hurt. Maisy could have been killed if that shrapnel had been a few inches higher."

Beneath his hand, Maisy shook, and he smoothed his hand across her back again to gentle her.

"We need to push. Harder. Faster before his next bomb kills someone," Miguel said, but before he could continue, a knock came at the door.

"Come in," he called out sharply, irritated at the interruption.

Liam opened the door cautiously, obviously sensing Miguel's impatience.

"We have something. I've cued it up on the computer for you to see," Liam said and gestured outside to their work area.

Miguel squashed his irritation and nodded. "Good work, Liam. We'll be there in a second." He turned to his team and said, "I'm sorry if I was abrupt, but leaving a bomb at our door is a challenge. He thinks he's smarter than us. That he can keep on terrorizing the city, but we will stop him."

"No doubt about that, Miguel. We will stop him," Madeline said, rose from the table and was followed by Nicholas and Dash, leaving Miguel alone with Maisy.

He leaned against the table so he could examine her better. A few bits of debris were tangled in the thick strands of her caramel hair and he brushed them away as he asked, "Are you okay? Really okay?"

Her gaze shimmered with unshed tears, but she stiffened her lips and nodded. "A little sore. Arm hurts like crazy, but okay. Alive," she said with a rough breath.

"He won't get to you again. I promise you that. I won't let you out of my sight again," he said, but her smile turned rueful and she shook your head.

"You will because you have to get to work. Like now," she said and jerked her head in the direction of the door.

He hated that she was right. The job had to come first before anything else, including Maisy.

"Let's go," he said and quickly added, "please."

HE WAS RATTLED and Maisy understood why. Hell, she was absolutely terrified, but she knew that for the good of the investigation and for them—if there was a "them"—she had to stay calm.

They walked to the workspace where Madeline, Dashiell and Nicholas were already seated at the table. Liam stood off to the side at one of the computers and as Miguel and Maisy settled themselves at the table, he said, "About an hour before the blast, a group of what looks like homeless people walked by the building. Watch the man in the center of the group."

The projection monitor snapped to life and a video played showing a group of about half a dozen people approaching the building. They were coming from a nearby highway area and Maisy supposed that like at many other underpasses on the edges of the city, the homeless group had set up an encampment.

The video jumped to another angle, probably from another camera, Maisy thought.

This angle showed the same group, who strolled toward the column, surrounding one man as Liam had mentioned. His hood was up and there was something familiar about him. She pointed to him and said, "The one in the middle. That's his hoodie."

No sooner had she said that than the man slipped to the edge of the group with a black knapsack and placed it next to the pillar. As he did so, the hood fell back to reveal his face before he quickly jerked it back up.

"That's him! I know that's him!" she shouted and pointed to the picture as Liam froze the video.

"That's our man and quite young. Early twenties," Miguel said.

"Like the Austin Serial and Smiley Face Bombers," Nicholas said.

"We're already working on cleaning up the video and will start running it against the various databases," Liam said just as David walked over, a smile on his face.

Dash glanced at his intern and said, "I hope there's a reason for that smile."

Chapter Fifteen

"We didn't get a hit on CODIS, but we got a hit at the DNA testing service we can access. Not an exact match, but the individual in the database is likely a cousin," David said.

Miguel dipped his head and said, "Excellent work. Please get us whatever information you can on that individual so we can interview them."

"Will do," David said and headed back to his computer to work.

Miguel turned his attention to the team. "Nicholas, I need you to get back on the street to interview the other licensed blasters on our list. Madeline, please work with Dash and Liam on that list of possible suspects. Hopefully with the new photos of the unsub, we'll be able to at least limit the list. In the meantime, I'm going to take Maisy home so she can rest. I'll be back later."

"That's not necessary, Miguel," Maisy said, a stain of color on her cheeks, as if she was embarrassed by his concern.

"But it is. I want to make sure that you're safe, not

like before," he said and skipped his gaze across his team members to see if anyone disagreed.

"This latest bomb could have been specifically set because the Crusader knew that Maisy would be here," Nicholas said.

Miguel appreciated his support. "Anything happens, call, text or email. I'll be working at my place."

He glanced at Maisy, almost daring her to contradict him in front of his team again, but she remained silent. Slowly she rose, wincing as she did so, making him slip his arm around her waist to offer support.

She shrugged off his assistance, obviously upset with him.

He got it, but that wasn't going to make him change his mind. Together they walked out of the BAU offices, to the elevator and down to his condo. No words were exchanged. In fact, she avoided his gaze, clearly still annoyed with him.

They had no sooner stepped inside his condo when she whirled on him. "I appreciate your concern, but you have a job to do."

He blew out an exasperated sigh and dragged a hand through his hair. "My job is to protect you."

She jabbed him in the chest with a very pointy index finger. "Your job is to catch the Seattle Crusader. That's how you'll keep me and tons of others safe."

He couldn't argue with her, but he did. "And do you think I can keep my mind on this investigation if I don't know that you're safe? The entire time I was with Nicholas earlier, all I could think about was whether you were okay."

His revelation obviously surprised her. "You were thinking about me?"

With a heavy sigh, he looked away and said, "I was."

She cradled his cheek and gently urged him back to face her. "I was thinking about you, too, but I don't think that's a good thing for either of us, is it?"

"No, it isn't. We both want different things from life," he admitted.

"We do, but if we want to get on with our lives, you need to trap this terrorist. You can't do that holed up with me here."

He hated that she was right. Worse, he hated that even though she was right, he was still worried about the prospect of leaving her here alone. After all, the Crusader had struck right on their doorstep, almost as if to taunt them that both Maisy and the FBI weren't safe.

But he had to leave her, as much as he might not like it.

"Why don't you take a shower to relax? You're probably sore from being tossed around."

"I am. Again," she said with a wry smile and a short chuff of a laugh.

"I'll have another agent at the door until I come back," he said and before he could stop himself, he dropped a quick kiss on her lips.

MAISY WAS SURPRISED by his show of affection, and worse, she wanted more than just that brief touch.

But that would only complicate things even more as they had both said.

They wanted different things from life and yet…

She wouldn't think about how tempting it was to imagine having a life with Miguel. To share it and bring him the peace he was missing. The life he was missing by living here at work.

"¡Cuídate!" she said and rushed off to shower and ease some of the pains in her body from being thrown by the blast.

The heat of the water helped ease some of the soreness and the waterproof bandage protected the gash on her arm. But as she swept her soapy hands across her body, she noted the assorted bruises from the first blast that were only just turning purplish and yellow as well as a few newer bruises.

She finished showering, wrapped a towel around her body and used another to create a makeshift turban around her hair. But when she exited the bathroom, she discovered that Miguel was still in the apartment. He sat at the kitchen table in front of his laptop, tapping away at the keys.

He raised his head as she walked in and explained.

"I can't get an agent here for another hour or more and the rest of the team is working on their assignments. If you feel up to it, would you mind going back up to the BAU offices with me?"

She was physically up to it, but emotionally… Every minute spent with Miguel made keeping her emotional distance from him harder. But she also didn't want to keep him from doing his job because the safety of others was at risk.

"I'm up to it. Just give me a few minutes to get ready," she said, rushed to her suitcase and pulled out clothes to wear. She hurried to the bathroom, where she dressed and with a few quick strokes through her hair, brushed out any tangles. It would air dry, curlier than normal but otherwise fine.

When she exited the bathroom, Miguel glanced in her direction again, but his look went from all business to something else. Something dangerous that ignited heat throughout her body.

"You're so beautiful," he said.

Heart beating heavily, she told herself to deflect, deflect, deflect. "Why, Supervisory Special Agent Peters, I bet you say that to all the girls."

He laughed as she intended and shook his head. "You are truly something. Seriously," he said and shot to his feet. "Let's go. Please."

She nodded and rushed to his side, and he laid a hand at her back to guide her toward the door. The touch was comforting. Possessive.

At the door, he said, "Please let me."

She paused as he wanted and he went to the door, opened it and looked around the hallway before extending a hand to confirm it was okay to exit.

Slipping her hand into his, she walked with him out the door and to the elevator but didn't release his hand, the touch uniting them in more than one way.

When they reached the offices, Dashiell was sharing high fives with Liam and David. Liam turned to face them as they walked to where Nicholas and Madeline were adding information to their white-board.

Miguel smiled as the enlargement of a Washington State driver's license went up next to the earlier, grainy photos they had created from the various CCTV feeds and Maisy's photo of the unsub.

"Good news, I guess," he said and pulled out a chair for Maisy to sit at the table.

"Good news," Dashiell confirmed and explained. "Using the program I tweaked, we were able to splice in more of the unsub's features from the CCTV footage and recreate his face. As soon as we did that, we got a hit. Chris Adams. Twenty-six. No priors. Last employer was none other than the city of Seattle. He worked in the parks department but was let go about six months ago."

Miguel peered around the room at his team. "Do we have anything else on Adams?"

Madeline shook her head. "Still working on it. We're reaching out to the cousin whose DNA hit earlier, but since his last name is Adams as well, we're confident we're on the right track. We've also identified two siblings who are currently serving time for armed robbery and drug dealing."

Miguel nodded. "Which would explain the Crusader's demands about bail reform and sentencing. What about his last known address?"

Nicholas held up a piece of paper. "Got it. I was

just about to go visit the location and see what I can find."

"I'll go with you. In the meantime, see what else you can dig up and also, let's get his last place of employment, address, et cetera up on the map and see if that gets us anywhere," he said and started to go, but then he laid a hand on Maisy's shoulder and gently squeezed it.

"You'll be okay here," he said, but it was part question, part statement.

"I will be. I just wish there was more I could do to help," she said, glancing up at him with those amazing eyes, trusting eyes. He hoped he didn't disappoint her again the way he had earlier when she'd been hurt.

"Okay. And team…good job. Reach out to Seattle PD, Mack at ABS and ATF Special Agent Cummings and fill them in on what we have. See if they have anything to add. Also ask for a BOLO on Chris Adams."

"I've got that," Madeline said, and Miguel had no doubt she'd have everything in line within minutes. It was why she was one of his best agents and working on his team.

"Thanks, Madeline." When they left the elevator bank and then headed out of the building, Miguel checked to make sure the area was safe. The Crusader had attacked on their home turf, reminded them that no one was safe anywhere.

That was doubly evident at the sight of the various first responder vehicles and news vans parked in front of the office building as well as the assorted officers working just past the yellow barricade tape at the blast scene.

As one of the reporters noticed them, she came running in their direction, and with a quick look at Nicholas, Miguel urged his team member to move a little faster. They beat the reporter to the car and were safely inside and pulling away from the reporter as she reached them.

"Vultures," Miguel mumbled beneath his breath.

"I don't blame you for not liking the press all that much," Nicholas said.

Miguel shrugged. "They can really have a negative impact on an investigation between revealing information and creating unnecessary pressure."

"Like in the Olympic Park Bomber case," Nicholas said, trying to understand how he felt.

He nodded. "Definitely. We can't risk naming an unsub unless we're one hundred percent sure about it."

"Which is why you haven't named Rothwell as an unsub?" Nicholas said, well aware of Miguel's suspicions about the annoying, and potentially dangerous, senate candidate.

"Especially Rothwell. If I say anything without having the proof to back it up, it's not fair to him or to my team," he said and shot a quick glance at the other man before returning his attention to the road.

NICHOLAS PEERED AT his boss as Miguel grew silent. He admired Miguel's restraint, even to someone as obnoxious as Rothwell. It was a testament to his character and his inherent sense of fairness, reinforcing the kind of man he was. A good man. An honorable man.

Nicholas wasn't sure he could be as restrained if someone he loved was at risk. Earlier that summer when he'd been trying to solve a serial killer case and fallen for the victim's older sister, he'd nearly lost his mind when Aubrey had been taken hostage by their unsub.

Although Miguel had been business as usual during this investigation, it was impossible to miss that there was a connection between him and Maisy, which worried him. Any distractions could prove fatal and today's bombing right on their doorstep was ample warning that they all needed to double their focus on this case.

Which was why he took the lead as they rang the bell for the superintendent when they reached the apartment building where Chris Adams had lived. The older Latino man immediately answered the door but narrowed his gaze warily as he spotted them. "Can I help you?"

They both held up their badges and identified themselves. "FBI. Special Agent Nicholas James and Supervisory Special Agent Miguel Peters. Are you Gonzalo Garcia, the building superintendent?"

The man's eyes widened in surprise. "*Sí*, I am. FBI? I don't understand."

Nicholas whipped out a copy of Chris Adams's

driver's license photo. "We understand this man used to live here."

The superintendent peered at the photo, nodded and then opened the door wide for them. "Please come in. It's better if we talk inside."

Nicholas and Miguel did as he asked and watched as the older man inspected the street before he closed the door.

"Is there a problem, Mr. Garcia?" Nicholas asked since the man was clearly spooked.

"Chris lived here about six months ago, but after he lost his job and fell behind on his rent, the landlord had me evict him," the superintendent said.

"Was he violent when he was evicted?" Miguel asked.

The man shook his head. "Not at first. But then Chris got involved with some of the homeless people down beneath the highway. They started coming around and causing problems. Turning over garbage cans or setting them on fire. Hassling tenants for money as they come and go to their cars. That's why I didn't want anyone to see us talking. I don't want no problems."

"Did you call the police about the incidents?" Nicholas asked even though he knew what the answer would be.

"I did, but their hands are tied. As long as no one gets hurt, we're on our own," Mr. Garcia said with a resigned shrug.

"You said Chris lost his job," Nicholas said, leaving it open-ended so the super could add anything he knew.

"Chris wasn't bad at first, but he partied a lot. I think he was high at work and someone got hurt so they fired him."

Nicholas and Miguel shared a look. "He was with the parks department, right?"

The super nodded. "He was. Worked mainly at Riverview, but also Denny Park. Some others, I think."

"Has Chris been around lately?" Nicholas pressed.

Mr. Garcia shook his head and frowned. "Not in the last couple of weeks. He had been staying down at the encampment beneath the highway overpass. I figured he either got himself another place or maybe overdosed or something. Shame, really."

"It is. If you think of anything else, or if you see Chris around, would you mind giving us a call?" Nicholas said and handed the man his business card.

The man tapped the card against his hand and nodded. "*Sí.* I will."

They left the superintendent's apartment and walked away from the building, perusing the area as they moved toward the highway overpass. It was several blocks away, but quite a number of homeless could be seen through the area and a few tents had been pitched here and there along the edges of the public sidewalks. The closer they got, the denser the appearance of tents and makeshift lodgings.

As they passed, people stared at them and Nicholas suspected that even if Chris was still hanging around the encampment, they wouldn't get any help in finding him. That was confirmed as they walked over to one person after another. They either hurried away, avoiding them, or refused to answer. Another, smaller group of more aggressive people moved as if to surround them, but Nicholas held his hands up in surrender and he and Miguel turned around and walked back to their car.

"We'll need to set up surveillance around the encampment," Miguel said as he slipped behind the wheel.

"I can do that with David. He wants to be a field agent and it'll be good experience for him," Nicholas said.

Miguel nodded. "Sounds good. Maybe after we get back you can both change into something less law enforcement and see if that helps at all."

Nicholas replayed in his head what the superintendent had told them, one fact sticking out. "He mentioned Denny Park. Isn't that close to the federal courthouse?"

"And some parts of Riverview are not all that far from some of the bombing sites. Same for this encampment and his old apartment," Miguel said, but instead of driving directly to the BAU offices, he detoured by Riverview and then up to the area by the courthouse and the park.

"Do you see what I see?" Miguel asked as they drove past a corporate park and one headquarters stood out: Rothwell Industries.

"I do," Nicholas said and didn't fail to notice his

boss's smile. With every bit of information they uncovered, they were getting closer and closer to finding out who was the real Seattle Crusader, and he
suspected that it wasn't going to be just Chris Adams.

Chapter Sixteen

Maisy nursed the tea that she had prepped for herself while Madeline added even more information to the team's whiteboard.

"Do you think you're getting closer to catching the Crusader?" she asked and sipped her tea.

Madeline leaned her hands on her hips as she peered at the board. The action drew the jacket away from her athletic physique and revealed the weapon tucked into a black leather holster. She tilted her head as she considered the evidence she had just written onto the whiteboard and nodded.

"I think we have one of the Crusader's minions," she said and turned to face Maisy. "I'm sure someone else is directing him and making the bombs."

Maisy considered the information and nodded. "Adams doesn't seem like the mastermind type to me."

"Your father… Sorry, the Forest Conservation Bomber said our unsub is a novice and I totally agree. I also think that there's another reason for these bombings. Not the demands for bail reform and homeless encampments."

"You think that it's a smoke screen?" Maisy wondered aloud.

"Definitely a smoke screen," Miguel said as he hurried in with Dashiell and walked straight to the whiteboard. He placed several red magnets on their map and gestured to them. "Adams's apartment, a homeless encampment where he's been seen and the location of a couple of the parks where he worked before being fired."

Miguel grabbed two other magnets and snapped them onto the whiteboard decisively. He pointed to the first one. "Federal courthouse where several riots have taken place, but more importantly," he said and gestured to the second spot, "the corporate offices of Rothwell Industries. Right near the park and courthouse."

Liam rose from his computer and walked over at the same time that Lorelai entered their work area. They nearly bumped into each other but jumped back, staring at each other uneasily as they both mumbled, "Sorry."

"You first," Liam said and held his hand out to cede the floor to her.

"No, you first. I was just coming to see if you wanted dinner brought in," Lorelai said.

"What do you have, Liam?" Miguel asked as Lorelai and Liam continued to do their awkward little dance.

Liam dipped his head in apology to Lorelai, walked over to Miguel and handed him some papers. A broad smile came to Miguel's lips and he shot a quick glance at Nicholas as he said, "The cousin has confirmed that he's related to Chris Adams, so we've got him thanks to the DNA evidence off the bombs."

Miguel's phone chirped to warn of an incoming text. He pulled it from his pocket, read the text and then jerked his head in Liam's direction. "Please put the TV feed up on the monitor."

Liam raced back to his computer, careful to avoid Lorelai, and with a few keystrokes, put up the feed of a press conference with none other than state senate candidate Richard Rothwell.

"It's a disgrace that the FBI continues to refuse my help. Especially considering that the latest bombing was right at their door," Rothwell said, his too-serious expression and tone almost comical.

"Smug bastard," Nicholas murmured.

"While I don't believe in caving to terrorists, we must consider that the Crusader's demands are intended to help so many. Issues like bail reform and the plight of the homeless are ones I intend to address once I'm elected to the Senate," he said, and a small cheer rose in the background.

The camera panned away from Rothwell to the crowd.

"You getting this, Liam?" Miguel asked.

"I am," their tech confirmed, but instead of returning to Rothwell, the reporter took over the broadcast.

"This is Allie Smith reporting from Rothwell Industries. Back to you, Ernie."

"And back to our investigation. Nicholas and David are going to the homeless encampment near Adams's old apartment. BOLO is out for him. In the meantime, let's keep working on busting past the shell companies. I'm convinced they're going to lead to Rothwell," Miguel said and as everyone rushed off to continue work and Lorelai went to order dinner, he came over, sat beside Maisy and brushed back a lock of hair that had fallen onto the side of her face.

"You holding up?" he asked, his gaze skimming over her features, searching out what she was feeling.

"I am. Tired. Sore. Hungry," she admitted with a laugh and a wag of her head.

"We'll go down to my apartment as soon as we finish dinner, unless you'd rather get something to eat on our own," he said.

Dinner alone with Miguel. Dangerous, she thought. "We can eat with the team. I'm sure you're anxious to be here if something happens so you can wind this up now that you have an unsub."

Miguel nodded and once again brushed his hand across his hair. "We have Adams, but I want whoever is directing this and whoever made those bombs."

She understood his determination while she was also sad that their time together would be coming to a close.

"You'll get them. I have no doubt about that," she said and laid her hand over his. Squeezed it gently.

"Your mother would be really proud of the work you're doing."

A sad smile flitted across his lips. "She would. She's the voice in my head, pressing me to do my best."

The moment was shattered as Lorelai returned to the work area with two FBI agents carrying bags from one of the nearby restaurants. The aroma of yeasty bread and sweet cream wafted into the air as Lorelai laid out assorted plastic food containers and bread bowls on the surface of their work area.

"I figured you were tired of sandwiches, and something warm would be nice. There are four different soups for you to choose from. If you don't need anything else, I'm going to head out," Lorelai said.

Liam piped up immediately, "Are you sure you don't want to stay and eat with us?"

Lorelai fidgeted, leaning side to side on her four-inch heels, but then she said, "No, thanks. I have a date."

Liam's face fell and Lorelai rushed from the room, obviously uncomfortable.

Miguel clearly got the tension between the two since he jumped to his feet, clapped his hands and said, "Let's eat."

MIGUEL'S BELLY WAS full of tasty seafood chowder and bread, but there was an emptiness inside that even the best gourmet food couldn't fill.

As Maisy sat back in her seat and rubbed her

stomach, a contented sigh escaped her and slipped into him, filling some of that void inside him. Warning him that maybe, just maybe, Maisy was what would fill the emptiness. An emptiness that he hadn't really acknowledged until she had come into his life.

Peering around the table, he noticed that the meal had relaxed his team members, which was a good thing. Sometimes too much tension blocked the flow of ideas, but so far, he was pleased with what his team had accomplished. But they still had a long way to go to resolve the investigation.

Despite that, it was time to get Maisy home and to enter his own zone because sometimes he worked better alone.

He slowly rose to his feet, wincing a bit as the stitches in his leg pulled with the motion. "I think it's time we went home. Keep me posted on any developments. I'm going to dig into Rothwell and see what I can find."

He held his hand out to help Maisy up and she slipped her hand into his. Inside him, another bit of the emptiness filled with the warmth of her skin and her tender squeeze.

But as aware as he was of every nuance of Maisy beside him, he didn't fail to notice how Madeline's eyebrows rose as she saw their held hands. How Dashiell likewise fixated on that while Liam crossed his arms, his gaze puzzled.

Miguel understood their concerns because he'd had similar ones as his team members had found their significant others during the course of their last few investigations. Nicholas and Aubrey. Madeline and Jackson. Dashiell and Raina. And of course, the ongoing drama between Liam and Lorelai, his ex.

He gazed at Maisy and thought, *Now it's my turn*.

With a light tug on Maisy's hand, he urged her from their work area, and they walked out of the offices, to the elevator and down to his apartment.

As soon as they were through the door, he released her hand and they stepped apart, gazing at each other, obviously uncomfortable. He broke the tension with a flip of his hand in the direction of the Murphy bed.

"I'm going to be working and you're probably sore. Maybe you should take the bed tonight so you're more comfortable."

She opened her mouth, as if to object, but then just nodded. Clasping her hands before her, she said, "Thanks. But there's room for you as well."

And there was the eight-hundred-pound gorilla in the room again, and he might as well address it. Walking up to her, he cradled her cheek and stroked his thumb across her creamy skin. So smooth. So soft. His gut tightened at the thought of all that skin against his and she was more than he could resist.

Bending closer, he brought his lips to hers until only the space of a breath was between them. "This," he said, whispered his lips across hers and shifted back barely an inch. "This is why that's not a good idea."

In answer, Maisy reached up and cupped the back

of his head, keeping him close. "This," she said, repeating his earlier action, her lips a butterfly kiss against his. "This is why we have to share that bed. Whatever happens, I don't want to say that I ran from this. From us."

A low groan escaped him, and he couldn't fight it anymore. He wrapped his arms around her and hugged her close, her softness crushed to his hardness. Every inch of her fitting to him as if they were two pieces of a puzzle.

Over and over they kissed, until their breaths became one and almost ceased to exist as they strained toward each other.

But then something registered. Sound. Vibration.

"Damn," he said and fumbled with the phone in his jacket pocket, dropping it with a thud.

That sound killed the desire as effectively as a cold bucket of water.

"SSA Peters," he said, and mouthed an apology to her.

"We've broken through one of the shell companies and like you thought, it's part of Rothwell Industries," Dashiell advised.

"That's great, Dash. We're one step closer to Rothwell. I'm sure he's the mastermind behind this," Miguel said.

"I agree, Miguel. We'll keep on working to break past the other shell. Hopefully it'll lead to Rothwell also."

"I don't doubt that it will and if we can get Adams

into custody, maybe he will flip on Rothwell. As for the licensed blaster, I think there's one on our list that's at Rothwell's current construction site. If you can get an address for him, I'll go with Madeline to interview him."

"We'll try to get it ASAP," Dashiell said and ended the call.

Miguel tossed the phone onto a nearby tabletop and it clattered noisily, making Maisy jump and take a step away from him.

"You need to get to work," she said and smoothed her hand across his chest.

"I do. Why don't you—"

The phone rang and vibrated noisily on the tabletop.

"Again?" Miguel muttered in frustration, swept up the phone and answered, "SSA Peters."

"We've got the address for the blaster from his license application and his photo from his driver's license," Madeline said.

"Great. Meet me in the lobby. We'll speak to him and see what he has to say," Miguel directed.

Facing Maisy, he said, "I have to go."

"I understand. I'll be waiting up for you."

The last bit of emptiness inside him disappeared at the thought of Maisy waiting for him at home. A home and not just a place to lay his head between investigations.

"That'll be nice. I'll make sure an agent is at the

door while I'm gone," he stated and rushed to the door, Maisy following.

At the door he faced her, bent and kissed her, a long, slow kiss filled with promise.

After they broke apart, Maisy smiled, cupped his cheek and swiped her thumb across his lips. *"¡Cuídate!"*

"You take care as well. Do not open this door for anyone."

"I won't," she said and when he stepped out, he heard the snap of the locks falling into place.

He immediately called up to the offices and arranged for an agent to come down. He didn't leave until he saw the agent come off the elevator and only then did he hurry to meet Madeline in the lobby.

She was scrolling through her phone, a happy smile on her face when he met her.

"How's Jackson?" he said, certain that was who had put the smile on Madeline's face.

Madeline laughed and flipped her phone so he could see the photo of Jackson and his six-year-old daughter, Emmy, happy faces streaked with flour as they showed off the batch of cookies they had apparently just baked. Just a month earlier, Madeline had been the lead agent when Emmy had been kidnapped during a Take Your Child to Work Day event at Jackson's office.

"Looks like things are back to normal after the kidnapping," he said and they walked together to Miguel's car, chatting.

"As normal as anyone can be after something like that," she said, some of her earlier happiness gone.

"I know it was a rough case for you, being so similar to when your sister was taken," he said, well aware that Madeline's case had not had such a happy ending.

"It was, but there was a silver lining. Meeting Jackson and his daughter…it's changed my life. I have a life," she said with a rough laugh, and then peered at him intently as they paused by his car.

"I think things are also changing for you. Or am I wrong to think that?" Madeline asked.

Miguel shrugged. "It's complicated and I know you can understand that," he said and slipped into the car.

Madeline joined him, in the passenger seat, and provided an address for the blaster's home in the Central District, an area which was one of the oldest residential neighborhoods in the city and which had seen quite a number of changes over the years. The neighborhood had a mix of homes and small businesses and had at one time been a predominantly African American neighborhood. Gentrification had changed that and led to a number of new construction sites as well as many resident-driven projects to improve the area's parks and schools.

"I understand that you're attracted to Maisy and I get it. She's a beautiful woman, but more importantly, she's brave and kind and caring," Madeline said as if she was arguing the case for Maisy.

"She is and I am. Attracted. But you more than most understand just how hard a job we have. The long and erratic hours. The cases that take their toll on your soul," he admitted.

"The cases can break you. The pain and suffering of the victims. The frustration that you can't solve the case fast enough to keep someone else from suffering," she said, totally in sync with him. But before he could say anything else, she continued, "Being with Jackson and Emmy…it's lightened that load. It's made it easier to deal with all that pain and suffering because I'm not alone anymore."

Just like I don't feel alone anymore, Miguel thought, but kept it to himself since they were nearing the edges of Central District and he had to focus on finding the address for the licensed blaster they were going to interview.

After a few turns, he pulled up in front of a small brick house on a block of mixed homes. Some had been renovated and sparkled brightly beside others that needed care, just like this home. One of the steps had cracked and fallen off to the side and the paint on the white trim around the windows was peeling. The downspout had pulled loose from the gutter, allowing water to pour down and stain the brick along that side of the home. A white wrought iron fence surrounded the property, rusting in spots and with a front gate that was slightly askew.

There was a light on, but curtains hid their view

past the older jalousie windows across the front of the house.

Miguel parked in front and killed the engine. They exited the car, but as they pushed the gate open, it squeaked loudly. Someone drew the curtain aside, as if to see who had come onto the property, and then let it fall back in place again. He shared a look with Madeline, who peeled off from him to walk to the edge of the fenced-in property so she could keep an eye on the backyard.

He walked up to the door and knocked. The muffled sound of voices came from behind the wooden door and then it opened just a crack. A woman stood on the other side. Mid-thirties and very pregnant from what little he could see past the small sliver of the opening.

Holding up his ID, he said, "FBI. Supervisory Special Agent Miguel Peters. I'd like to speak to Randy Davis. Is he available?"

"He's not home," she said, but at the same time, the thud of booted feet carried from behind her, followed by the slam of another door.

"He's running," Miguel shouted at Madeline, who rushed across one side of the yard while he raced down the stairs and to the other side.

He caught sight of a man sprinting across the yard in his direction and ran to cut him off. Before he could reach him, the man vaulted over the low wrought iron fence and raced across the neighboring yard. Miguel followed, grabbing hold of the fence to hurdle over it, but as he landed, his leg buckled a bit, still weak after the shooting. It sent him sprawling to the ground in a heap, but he pushed back onto his feet, giving chase in an awkward run, every other step filled with pain.

But Davis, their unsub, was fast and quickly disappeared from view.

He stopped, fists on his hips in frustration as Madeline caught up to him.

"I lost him. I couldn't keep up," he said with a rough breath.

"We'll get him," Madeline said and patted him on the back. The gesture was meant to console, but it only frustrated him even more.

"We will," he said and jerked out his phone to call Seattle PD. In no time he had arranged for a BOLO to be put out on Davis and police surveillance of the premises. Then he reached out to fill in Mack at ABS and the ATF special agent. With another call back to the BAU offices, he had Dashiell working on getting a search warrant so they could see what evidence would turn up at the blaster's home.

"Let's head back. Hopefully we'll have the warrant shortly and see if Rothwell is more than just Davis's employer," Miguel said and brushed some dirt off his suit as they returned to his sedan.

Once they were inside and heading back to the BAU offices, Madeline said, "I have to admit I thought you were a little off base when you pegged Rothwell

as being involved, but there are just too many connections to him."

Miguel took a quick look at her as he drove. "So
now you agree that he's part of this?"

With a shrug that barely shifted the fine wool of
her suit jacket, she said, "I think it's way more probable than not."

Miguel quickly ran down what they had so far,
intending to convince her that it was more than just
probable. "Two shell companies owned by him, since
I have no doubt the second one will be a Rothwell
property. The licensed blaster works at one of his
construction sites. Adams worked barely a block or
so from Rothwell's business office."

"All circumstantial," Madeline reminded him.

"For now. In time we'll get what we need to nail
him," Miguel said, more convinced than ever that
Rothwell was the mastermind behind the Seattle
Crusader.

With another shrug, Madeline said, "I hope you're
right and that we'll be able to get him before another
bombing hurts someone."

"I know we will."

Chapter Seventeen

Maisy couldn't sleep. She couldn't even get comfortable knowing that Miguel was out there, possibly in danger. That his team was out there, likewise risking their lives to keep others safe.

It made her wonder how the wives and husbands of the police, FBI and other first responders did this every day.

Could I do this every day? she wondered, but then forced her thoughts away from that.

Miguel and she had been thrown together by this investigation and it was unlikely that their relationship would become more after this terrorist had been caught.

So she had to grab whatever joy she could with both hands.

When Miguel walked in, limping slightly as he entered, she shot to her feet and hurried to his side. Seeing that his suit and shirt were smudged with dirt and grass stains, she ran her hands across his arms and chest, as if searching for any injuries.

"Are you okay?" she asked.

He cupped her cheek and strummed his thumb there. "I am. The licensed blaster ran off when we tried to question him, and I fell going over a fence to chase him."

"Your leg," she said, glancing down to see if he'd ripped his stitches again.

He mimicked her action, peering down at his leg, but there was no sign of any damage.

"It's fine and you're up late." He slipped his hand into hers and with a playful tug, drew her toward the bed.

"I couldn't sleep. Had too much on my mind. I was worried," she admitted and faced him as they stood by the edge of the bed.

"I wasn't in any danger, unlike you. It kills me that you were hurt today. That I failed you," he said and tenderly ran his hand along the bandage on her arm.

She smiled and cradled his jaw. "You didn't fail me or anyone else. I see how hard you and your team are working to catch the Crusader."

"And yet they are still free, because with the blaster running away, I'm totally sure that it's someone higher up directing Adams and the blaster."

"Rothwell?" she said.

He nodded, but then shook his head. "It's late. You should try and get some sleep."

"I don't know if I could, but what about you? Aren't you tired?" she said and urged him to sit on the edge of the bed with her.

"A little," he admitted, and she sensed his reluctance with the admission.

"Why don't you take a moment and rest?"

MIGUEL WAS BONE-TIRED and his leg was throbbing from the earlier pressure he had placed on it. But more than anything, he was tired in his soul at the prospect of coming home to an empty house. A house without Maisy.

He'd never felt that way before. The thought of being alone like that had never bothered him. Until now.

So even a few minutes of respite beside her would be an unexpected blessing before she was gone.

"Just a short break," he said, eased off his suit jacket and holster and laid them beside the bed. Then he removed his soiled shirt and toed off his shoes.

Maisy was resting against some pillows in the center of the bed and he scooted over and joined her there. Tucking her against his side, he leaned back and closed his eyes, savoring the moment.

She swept her hand across his T-shirt, her touch soothing, but he needed more than her comfort. He needed her in every way a man could need a woman.

"Maisy," he said and half turned toward her, meeting her gaze. Her blue eyes had darkened to almost violet and he had no doubt of her desire. It was there in her gaze and the trembling of her body beside him.

But he wouldn't push her if she wasn't ready. "Are you sure?"

"I am," she said, and as if to prove it, she pressed him down into the pillows and rose over him. Grabbed the hem of his T-shirt and drew it slowly up and over his head to bare him to her gaze.

"You are so handsome," she said and ran her hand across his chest again.

"And you're stunning." He cradled her breast and beneath his palm and the thin fabric of her pajama top, her nipple beaded into an even tighter nub.

He caressed her and she ran her hand across the length of him, yanking a needy moan from him. That sound shattered the last of their restraint.

She jerked at his pants, wanting him free of them as much as he needed to see her bare and beneath him.

He got his wish a second later as she lay back and took him with her, inviting him to join her. To be one with her.

But he didn't want to rush. Didn't want to miss a second of being with her, this precious gift that he'd been given by fate.

He took his time, showing her with his hands and lips how much he treasured her, kissing and caressing her body until she was quivering beneath him. Clutching at him as her body rose ever higher toward a release.

When he eased his hand between her body to find her center, pleasure her, her climax ripped through her.

She called out his name and gripped his shoulders.

Shifted her hips along his erection and he couldn't hold back any longer. He fumbled for only a moment to slip on a condom, and then he drove into her, pausing to savor the feel of her warmth and tightness. So tight.

"Maisy, *mi amor*—" he began, but she covered his mouth with her hand and murmured, "Love me, Miguel. Love me."

He did, driving into her. Kissing her as he moved, drawing her higher and higher. Climbing with her until it was impossible to hold back and he fell over, losing himself in her. Accepting her loving cry of satisfaction as she joined him.

Falling down onto her, he eased to her side slightly and at her protest, he said, "I'm too heavy."

She wrapped her arms around him and smiled. "You're just right."

And for the first time since his mother's murder, he felt right. Felt at peace with her beside him.

But then the muffled sound of his phone came from his suit jacket and he knew.

This moment of peace was over.

NICHOLAS AND DAVID kept their distance as they spotted someone who matched Chris Adams's description slipping out of a tent and heading away from the highway.

They'd been on their feet most of the day, trying rather unsuccessfully to get help from the legion of homeless in various encampments.

They had started at the one closest to Adams's last known location, striking out time and time again since no one wanted to help them. After stopping for a quick bite for dinner, they'd actually found one helpful soul who had directed them to the Riverview Playfield and the nearby highway area.

"My sister was in King Street Station when that bomb went off. We were lucky she wasn't hurt," the man had told them after providing the information.

"We appreciate the help," Nicholas had said and headed to Riverview.

It was dark by the time they reached the park, and the ball fields and playground were empty. A number of trails ran from the playfields to some wooded areas and while they'd thought it was possible that Adams might have pitched a tent there, their informant had pointed them in the direction of the highway area.

Armed with that, they'd started a search of some of the homeless camps in and around the roadway, but with little success and cooperation.

Near midnight, they'd spotted their possible suspect, but hung back, unable to positively identify him in the dark. But as he passed beneath one streetlight and the smallest sliver of his face was visible, Nicholas had no doubt it was Chris Adams.

He laid a hand on David's arm to instruct him to hold up and pulled out his cell phone to call Miguel.

It took a few rings for his SSA to answer, not a usual occurrence.

"Yes, Nicholas," Miguel prompted.

"We have eyes on our unsub. He's just left a tent near the intersection of the 509 and West Marginal Way South and now he's heading south on First Avenue South."

"Great. Text us a link to track you and we'll meet you there," he said.

"Will do." He sent Miguel a text with a link to their location so he could follow where they were going.

Shoulders hunched, face hidden beneath a black hoodie, their unsub continued on the street, passing by a number of industrial buildings and a site where multicolored steel barrels were piled high behind a chain-link fence. Their unsub pushed on until he reached a break between properties and a fenced-in yard holding a number of forklifts, pallet trucks, scaffolding and other construction supplies.

"Rothwell's?" David asked as they hurried their pace to not lose track of Adams because the area between the two buildings was relatively dark.

"Possibly," he said since there was no identifying signage on the property.

When they neared the end of one building, they caught sight of Adams approaching a dark-colored, pricey sedan parked just beyond the edge of the fenced-in yard. The nose of the car faced forward, making it impossible for them to see who was behind the wheel or if anyone was even in the car.

As Adams hurried toward the passenger's side of

the car, they likewise sped up, hoping to get a better look.

They were close enough to snap off a photo when the car shot off in the direction of the Duwamish Waterway.

"Damn," Nicholas cursed as he and David gave chase on foot. The car quickly moved away from them, but not before Nicholas confirmed the license plate he had seen earlier.

MIGUEL RACED TOWARD the location the tracker had provided, Maisy at his side. Madeline and Dashiell were in a second vehicle just moments behind them.

The phone rang and seeing Nicholas's number in the caller ID, he immediately picked up.

"Adams just got into a dark, late-model sedan. Jaguar, I think. The license plate read Vote Roth. They were headed east toward the Duwamish."

"We're almost there," he said and shot a glance toward the GPS. "I think we can head him off on South Holden. Meet us there."

"Roger that," Nicholas said, and Miguel immediately called Madeline and Dashiell to provide an update and instructions.

"We're headed to South Holden, but if we miss him there, he could try to make a run for it by South Donavan," he said, and Madeline completely understood.

"We'll try to cut him off, but keep us posted," Madeline advised.

"Do you think we'll get him?" Maisy asked, but as he took a turn sharply, she braced her hands on the door and seat beside her.

"You okay?" he asked, worried for her safety even though Maisy had insisted on coming with him, determined to see the investigation through to the very end.

"Yes. Is it him? Is it Rothwell?" she asked, anger sharp in her tones.

"It seems that way," he said and took another rough turn that led them down the highway toward Nicholas's location. As they reached the street, Nicholas and David were waving them down on the highway.

He jerked the car to a stop and his team members hopped in. "No sign of them here, so he must be headed to South Park," David said, leaning forward to speak to Miguel.

"Please call Madeline and let her know," he said, intent on focusing on the drive and keeping an eye out for their unsub's car. He headed toward the waterway, hoping to pick up their trail as Madeline and Dashiell shot past them, staying on the road to try to head them off at the next entrance to the maze of industrial and factory sites in the area.

MADELINE PRESSED THE pedal to the metal and streaked by Miguel and the rest of the team to try to reach the next exit for the industrial area.

"If the unsub headed toward the waterway, we

may be able to head straight at them," she said and executed a harsh turn, wheels squealing to push them in the direction of the water.

They had barely gone two blocks when twin beams of light erupted from a side street.

Almost colliding with the car as it jumped into the intersection, Madeline screeched to a halt. A second later, the driver of the sedan, seeing that escape was blocked off in that direction, whipped back toward the water, likely trying to double back to freedom.

Madeline gave chase while Dashiell called the rest of the team, hoping that they'd be able to box him in.

"We're headed toward the marina," Dashiell said, his attention half on the road and the map on the GPS system.

"On it," Miguel said, but as they neared the water and the sight of masts and boats by the marina, the unsub's sedan veered wildly to the left and right and a sudden blast of light erupted inside the car. The sedan jerked to a halt, and the passenger's side door shot open. A man stumbled out, clutching his midsection.

The sedan peeled away while the man crumpled to the ground, clearly injured.

Dashiell was immediately on it as Madeline drove to the man and stopped the car.

A second later, Miguel pulled up, but Madeline waved him in the direction of the sedan, which was clearly disappearing down the street again. "He's heading toward the highway. I think he shot Adams."

Miguel nodded. "Call it in and keep us posted," he said and took off after the sedan.

Madeline rushed over to where Dashiell was tending to the injured man—Chris Adams without a doubt. She called for an ambulance and then knelt beside Adams, trying to offer comfort and get information while Dashiell tried to stem the flow of blood from the abdominal wound.

Too much blood, she thought.

Chapter Eighteen

The red taillights of the car were only a couple of blocks ahead of him but shooting straight for the exit to the highway.

Maisy was holding tight to the dash and front seat as they fishtailed from the side street onto the highway. In the dark of night, there was luckily little traffic, allowing him to keep an eye on the unsub's car.

From the back seat he heard Nicholas calling in to Seattle PD for backup and pinpointing their location as they sped onto the 99. There was more traffic there, forcing the unsub to weave in and out of slower-moving cars to make his escape. Miguel was worried that they could cause an accident, especially as a duo of Seattle PD cars swept onto the highway and joined them in the pursuit.

Miguel actually fell back, letting the police cruisers take the lead and also have the freedom to thread the needle and stay on the unsub's tail. Barely a mile later, another police cruiser jumped onto the highway and worked its way in front of the unsub's car in an attempt to box him in between the three cruisers giving chase.

Suddenly, the dark sedan stopped short, forcing two of the cruisers to peel away to avoid rear-ending it. In another surprise move, it shot almost directly across the highway to an exit and rushed off, leaving Miguel as the only vehicle that could follow.

"Hold on," he said, their sedan nearly flying over a bump on the exit and back onto one of the side streets.

Luckily, the police had called it in and no sooner had the unsub's sedan hit the access road for the highway than a cruiser was there, blocking the road.

With another sharp, almost two-wheeled turn, the sedan whipped onto a side street.

Miguel followed, his gaze locked on the unsub's taillights and on the nav system which showed that the sedan was headed into a dead end close to the Duwamish River. A quick look in the rearview mirror revealed the flashing lights of a police vehicle and the wail of sirens just ahead of them said they were closing the noose around their unsub.

Barely fifty yards ahead, the moonlight gleamed over the waters of the river. As the driver realized there was nowhere else to go, the car slammed to a stop at an awkward angle. The driver's side door flew open, but a cruiser was already there.

Two policemen threw their doors open and drew their weapons as Miguel pulled up. Not seconds later, a second police car drove up, followed by a television news crew who must have been listening to the police radio.

The reporter and cameraman were already filming as Miguel and Nicholas approached, guns drawn, David and Maisy trailing behind them.

"FBI. He's armed," Miguel called out and flashed his badge at the police officers, who had their weapons trained on the sedan.

"Toss your weapon and come out with your hands up," he instructed, but hung back, aware that the unsub may have already killed someone just minutes earlier.

The gun rattled against the pavement as the driver tossed it out. A second later, a familiar voice said, "I'm not armed."

"Step out with your hands on your head," Miguel said, expectant. Sure of who would exit the sedan.

A second later, Rothwell's salt-and-pepper head of hair popped out, squashed by his interlaced hands as Miguel had requested. The senate candidate stumbled a bit to exit the low-slung sedan, but then he stood, fully visible to one and all, especially the news team.

Justice, Miguel thought as he silently instructed Nicholas to keep his weapon trained on Rothwell while he walked over and handcuffed him. By then a second news team had hit the scene and Miguel schooled his features as he read Rothwell his Miranda rights.

Rothwell said nothing, just nodded, but it would

be enough, especially with all the cameras rolling to capture the moment.

Miguel escorted Rothwell to the police cruiser and turned him over to the custody of Seattle PD. "Lock him up. No one is to interview him without us. If he asks for a lawyer, give him his mandatory call, but let us know."

"We understand. We just got word that Adams is at Harborview. Your agents are with him," the one officer said as they took custody of Rothwell.

"We'll head there now," Miguel said and walked toward where Maisy, Nicholas and David waited by his vehicle.

As he did so, he was besieged by the reporters who had arrived on the scene. A reporter shoved a microphone almost into his face and he patiently eased it back.

"Can you confirm that state senate candidate Rothwell is the Seattle Crusader?" the reporter asked.

"Our investigation is still pending. We have no comment at this time," he said and pressed past the news crews to Maisy and his team.

When he got to her side, she said in tones only loud enough for him to hear, "Is it over?"

Sadly, he had no doubt it was. What was left was for them to pull together all that they already had plus whatever Adams and the blaster could provide to make their case bulletproof.

Which meant he and Maisy would go their separate ways as well.

"It is," he said and forced himself to look away from her crestfallen expression since she also seemed to understand what that meant.

He opened her door and helped her into the car and as he passed by Nicholas, his team member shot him a questioning look.

Miguel ignored it, focusing on what he would need to do at the hospital in order to get the evidence to not only charge Rothwell, but eventually secure a conviction.

Once they were in the car, he sped toward Harborview Medical Center, and thanks to the late hour, they were entering the ER area barely fifteen minutes later. Madeline and Dashiell were walking down the hall with a doctor, heads bent toward each other as they apparently discussed the status of their suspect.

Madeline noticed him immediately as they entered the waiting area and strode to him, a deep frown marring the perfection of her skin.

"Not good, I gather," he said when Dashiell joined them a second later.

"The bullet nicked an abdominal artery, and he lost a lot of blood. He's in surgery to repair the damage and it's touch and go," she said.

"Hopefully he'll pull through," Miguel said and had to ask the hard question. "Were you able to get anything out of him?"

"We did," Dashiell said. "Apparently Adams approached Rothwell a few weeks ago near his offices since he knew Rothwell was a candidate. They chatted about prison reform on account of the troubles that Adams's brothers had had."

Almost like a tag team, Madeline continued with the report. "A couple of weeks after that, Rothwell approached Adams and offered him some money and to help Adams with his brothers' sentences. Adams took the bait, but that's all we were able to get out of him before he passed out from blood loss."

Miguel dragged a hand through his hair in frustration, but there was little they could do about Adams except pray that he made it through the surgery. If he did, they might be able to get more information from him to close the book on Rothwell.

And thinking about Rothwell… "We'll pray that Adams survives the surgery. In the meantime, we need to go interview our erstwhile state senate candidate to see what he has to say."

Maisy's hand slipped into his and drew his attention. "Adams will make it. We have to believe that so you can put Rothwell away."

He forced a smile and nodded. "Hopefully."

Dashiell held up a small laboratory vial. "This may help. It's the bullet the ER doctor removed. Hopefully its ballistics will match any gun Rothwell handled."

Miguel took the vial and held it up to the light to

examine it. "He tossed out a 9 mm Glock and this definitely looks like the same caliber."

He pulled an evidence bag out of his pocket and tucked the vial into the bag. "Let's go speak to Rothwell."

BY THE TIME they reached the police station barely fifteen minutes later, Rothwell had already lawyered up and wasn't talking.

You could almost touch the tension in the interrogation room as Miguel and Nicholas sat across the table from Rothwell and his counsel. David and Maisy were waiting outside for them while a trio of Seattle detectives was in the space behind the one-way mirror, watching the interview.

"Richard, I can call you Richard, can't I?" Miguel said, determined to try to convince the politician to speak despite his having lawyered up.

"SSA Peters, Mr. Rothwell has already indicated that he has no interest in chatting with you," the lawyer said, his tone as smarmy as Rothwell's had been during his various television interviews.

"You understand that Mr. Adams has already admitted that your client hired him to take part in the Seattle Crusader bombings. Mr. Rothwell owns two of the locations where the bombings occurred. We have a gun that was fired by Mr. Rothwell—"

"My client advised me that it was Mr. Adams who pulled the gun on my client and he was only trying to defend himself when the gun went off."

"Which begs the question of why Mr. Adams was even in the car with your client," Nicholas pressed.

"Mr. Adams approached my client and offered to stop the bombings in exchange for the payment of one hundred thousand dollars. As a concerned citizen, my client agreed to meet with him to see if he couldn't convince Mr. Adams to turn himself in," the lawyer said and shot a quick look at his client, who was still sitting there silently. His arms were across his chest, an almost bored look on his face, infuriating Miguel.

He glared at Rothwell, ignoring his counsel as he said, "We know you hired Adams. We know you shot him to shut him up. The licensed blaster at your current construction project is on the run, but I bet that when we get him, and we will get him, he'll confirm that you were the one directing this terrorist campaign."

"As we've already said, my client was trying to stop Mr. Adams from committing any additional crimes," the lawyer insisted.

"And we'll prove otherwise and when we do, we're going to press for the maximum penalty of life imprisonment under the Patriot Act unless we get some cooperation from your client," Miguel said and at that, Rothwell's lawyer finally showed some concern.

"If you'll give us a moment," the lawyer said.

"Of course," Miguel said, rose and left the room, Nicholas following him out into the hallway.

A second later, the detectives came out of the nearby viewing room, and another police officer approached.

"What is it, Sergeant Lewis?" the one detective asked the uniformed officer.

"A Randy Davis turned himself in to custody a few minutes ago. He wants to speak to the FBI."

Miguel smiled and peered at Nicholas. "Rothwell's blaster. The net is closing on that arrogant bastard."

"It is. Time to let him and his counsel stew in there while we chat with Davis," Nicholas said.

Miguel nodded, but then peered toward Maisy and David, who were still sitting on the bench outside the interrogation room, patiently waiting. But if they were going to interview Davis and then Rothwell again, it might be hours before they were done.

He held up a finger and walked over to Maisy and David, knelt before them. She held a hand out to him and he took it, tenderly squeezed. "We are going to be here for some time. Maybe you should go back to my apartment."

"I can drive her back," David offered.

Miguel nodded, dug into his pants pocket and handed over his car keys to the young tech intern.

"Thank you, and David, you can head home afterward. I don't think we'll need you until the morning when we can hopefully tie up all the loose ends," Miguel said.

"Are you sure? I don't mind waiting," Maisy said

and tightened her hold on his hand, as if fearful that once she let go…

He didn't want to think about letting her go, but come morning, or the morning of the following day, that's what he would have to do. He'd have to let her go.

"I'm sure. Don't wait up for me," he said and despite his better judgment, he leaned close and brushed a kiss across her cheek.

"Thanks for taking her home, David," he said and meant it. She was going home. His home, and he didn't want to think any more about how that might change in just a short time.

He needed to think about what to do next in regard to Davis, the licensed blaster, and Rothwell. Adams as well, which prompted him to dial Madeline as David and Maisy walked away.

Maisy cast him one last forlorn look as they turned a corner to exit the police station, but then she was gone.

"Miguel. You there?" Madeline asked.

"Yes, yes, I am," he said, turning back to the moment at hand.

"Any news on Adams?"

"He's pulled through surgery. They have him in surgical ICU but are hopeful that they'll be able to move him to a regular room by the morning," Madeline said.

"That's good news. Maybe once he's stable, we can get more information from him."

"We'll be here, waiting to interview him," Madeline said.

He had no doubt that Madeline and Dashiell would stay until they had what they needed to get Rothwell.

"Thank you and try to get some rest," he said and ended the call.

Turning toward Nicholas and the detectives, he announced, "Time to interview Davis."

Chapter Nineteen

Maisy had changed and slipped into bed once she got back to Miguel's apartment, but she couldn't sleep.

She turned on the television and almost every station had breaking news reports about Rothwell's arrest. The news crews that had tracked them to the marina were running video of the politician's capture and her heart leaped in her chest at the sight of Miguel, gun drawn until Rothwell had tossed out his weapon.

He risked his life for her and for others. A true hero.

A lonely one, she thought, taking what might be a last look around the sterile apartment. Only there was something not as solitary about it in the days she'd been there. On the counter there were two mugs, waiting for their morning dose of coffee. Her computer, journal and some pens rested on the coffee table, calling for her attention, only she didn't feel like writing at the moment. Her heart was too heavy with what would happen now that the investigation was almost over.

She surfed through the channels, avoiding those running reports on the Seattle Crusader. Finally, she found a channel with a travel show and snuggled down to watch, imagining herself visiting the locations, cruising down the Danube from Budapest to Belgrade while lounging on a chaise on the deck of the boat.

Maybe one day, she thought as her eyes grew heavy lidded, but when the door opened and Miguel walked in, all other thoughts fled her brain.

He came straight away and sat on the bed, smudges as dark as charcoal beneath his brown eyes. He settled his gaze on her and said, "You're still awake."

She shrugged. "I couldn't sleep so I turned on the TV. All the news channels were running stories on Rothwell."

He nodded and undid his tie. "It'll only get worse in the next few days. There's blood in the water and the sharks will be circling."

Maisy sat up, clutching the bed covers to her, almost defensively. She didn't know why since Miguel had seen all of her anyway earlier that night.

He noticed the gesture and said, "I still need to do some work. I'll just take a nap on the couch."

"You need to rest. You look like you could drop," she said and cradled his cheek. His skin was rough with a thick evening beard and she ran her thumb across it. The rasp seemed overly loud in the quiet of late night. Even louder than the television on across the room.

Miguel seemed to sense the tension in her. He covered her hand with his. "It's going to be okay,

Maisy. We offered the licensed blaster immunity and he testified that Rothwell pressured him to provide the dynamite and wire."

"What kind of pressure would make someone do that?" she wondered aloud.

With a dip of his head, Miguel said, "Davis's wife is pregnant and on bed rest. It hit them hard financially and Rothwell said he'd fire him if he didn't cooperate. Once he did, however, Rothwell threatened to tell police he was the Crusader."

"Davis and Adams. They were just pawns in Rothwell's little game, just like my mother and me," she said, anger rising up at Rothwell and the many lives he had ruined with his actions.

"Not like you at all. I think you would have been strong enough to stand up to Rothwell," he said and drew her close, offering comfort with his embrace, but she wanted more than comfort from him tonight.

She wanted to be with him one last time because she knew that come morning, the clock would be ticking on their relationship.

Sweeping her hand beneath his suit jacket, she helped him ease it off, her hands trembling as she restrained herself. But then he jerked off his holster, seemingly as impatient as she was. Suddenly in a rush, they tossed off clothes and sank beneath the bedcovers together, everything else forgotten except being together before the morning came.

She urged him on with the gentle caress of her hands, bringing him close. Straining toward him because she wanted every inch of her body tight to his, as if to imprint that memory on her brain and skin.

THE WEARINESS THAT Miguel had felt as he'd walked in had vanished the moment she'd laid her trembling hands on him.

He moved in her, joined with her emotionally and physically. Wishing to hold on to that connection even as he pushed them ever closer to a release. Taking her breath into his, the scent of her as the musk of their lovemaking perfumed the air.

She arched beneath him and dug her fingers into his shoulders as she came, the bite of her nails a reminder of the pain he'd feel when she was out of his life.

"I love you," she cried out, her body quivering against his, and he lost it.

"I love you, too," he said and buried himself deep, his body shuddering as his release slammed into him.

He eased to her side and took her into his arms, not wanting to miss a minute of being with her. His breath still choppy as hers was, until little by little it lengthened, the trauma and labors of the day stealing him away to rest.

To dream of what it might be like if every night could be spent in the love and comfort of her arms.

IT SEEMED TO Maisy that she had barely fallen asleep when the noise of the shower dragged her awake.

Her body was still slightly sore, especially the

area around the gash on her arm where the shrapnel had injured her.

But that pain was nothing compared to the ache in her chest at what might happen today. However, the pain was balanced by the possibility that Seattle and its people would be safe from the terror created by the Seattle Crusader.

She slipped out of bed and grabbed some clothes just as Miguel came out of the shower, a towel wrapped around his lean hips, droplets of water glistening on his skin. He rubbed another towel against his head to dry his hair and when he was done, the short strands stood in a disarray of spikes.

"Good morning," he said, his voice rough.

"Good morning. I'm just going to take a shower," she said and rushed away, afraid that if she said anything more, she would fall apart.

MIGUEL WATCHED MAISY rush off and he understood.

Whatever had happened yesterday between them had been amazing. But today he had to deal with the reality that they might close the Seattle Crusader case and once they did that…

He rushed and dressed, needing to get up to the BAU offices to assemble all the evidence that they had and anything else that Liam might have found while the rest of the team had been chasing after Adams and Davis.

Which reminded him that he needed an update

on Adams's condition. It had been a few hours since the last message Madeline had sent him.

"Good morning, Miguel," she said, the tone of her voice a weird mix of cheery and exhausted.

"Is it a good morning?" he asked.

"Adams was moved to a private room about half an hour ago. Seattle PD is guarding him, and we were just heading there to see if he was able to talk to us."

"Keep me posted," he said and busied himself with making coffee while Maisy showered and dressed.

He had just finished prepping to-go cups for them when she came out of the bathroom, the wet strands of her hair framing her gorgeous face and those unforgettable blue eyes.

"Are you ready?" he asked, the simple question loaded with so much meaning.

"Ready as I'll ever be," she responded and together they headed up to the BAU offices.

When they entered, Nicholas was at their whiteboard, filling in the information they had gotten the night before from their unsubs.

As he shot a quick look at the board, he thought they had enough evidence to support charges against Rothwell and Adams, especially with the licensed blaster agreeing to testify in exchange for immunity. But he wanted the case to be bulletproof and with Davis getting immunity, a good attorney would try to downplay his testimony by arguing that Davis would say anything to avoid prison time.

Which meant they needed every bit of evidence they could get.

He guided Maisy to the table and noticed that Liam was at his computer, wearing the same clothes that he'd had on the day before.

He walked over and clapped Liam on the back. "Have you been here all night?"

Liam glanced up at him, eyes bleary with exhaustion. "I have, but I think you'll be happy with what I've found out."

"Why don't you come and fill us in and then head home," he said, but a second later, Lorelai walked in and shot a worried glance at Liam.

"You don't look too good," she said and went to his side. She brushed her hand across the short strands of his light brown hair, the gesture loving and dragging a smile from Liam.

"I'll be okay," he said and lovingly laid a hand on Lorelai's slender waist, but she jerked back, the earlier tenderness gone.

She was all business as she said, "Director Branson has seen the news and has asked that you call her and provide a report on where you stand with the investigation."

Miguel eyed Liam. "Are you ready to add your input to the report?"

Liam nodded. "Totally ready."

"I'll set up the video call," Lorelai said and marched away, her stilettos snapping against the tiled floor.

Liam tracked her departure and smiled sadly. "I'm a fool," he muttered.

As Miguel glanced toward their work area, his gaze fixed on Maisy and he muttered, "You're not the only one."

He didn't wait for Liam's reply, although the tech guru followed him to the main work area so he could provide his report as part of the update to Director Branson.

The ever efficient Lorelai pressed several buttons and a second later the video feed from his boss jumped onto the projection monitor at the front of the room.

"Good morning, Olivia," Miguel said.

Olivia nodded. "Good morning. I see from the news reports that we have several suspects in custody. Do you have anything to add?"

"Rothwell is being held by Seattle PD along with a licensed blaster who worked for him. We've given Davis, the blaster, immunity in exchange for his testimony. Chris Adams, the individual who actually placed the bombs at the various locations, is in the hospital. Special Agents Striker and West are waiting to conduct an additional interview with him, but Adams has confirmed that Rothwell hired him to do the bombings. It appears Rothwell himself made the bombs, but we're going to need additional physical evidence to prove that," Miguel advised and then looked toward Liam. He gestured to him and said, "Agent McDare has some information for us."

Liam stepped forward. "We had tracked one shell company to Rothwell, but I was able to also connect the second shell company to him. More importantly, it appears that Rothwell has placed insurance claims for both of the properties which were damaged."

Olivia nodded. "So in addition to using the bombings to possibly improve his public perception during his campaign, he's benefitting financially as well."

"It seems that way. We'll work on getting a search warrant of his various properties to see if we can turn up any other evidence. In the meantime, we're preparing our report so that the U.S. attorney can review the cases against the various individuals and proceed with action as is appropriate," he said.

"Wonderful news, Miguel, and thank you to all the team members. I'll report to the FBI director. If there are any other developments, please keep me posted," she said, a broad smile on her features before she ended the video call.

Miguel faced his team and Maisy, likewise smiling. "You've all done a great job, but now we have to tie up any loose ends so that the case the government presents is airtight."

"I'll keep on digging," Liam said, but Miguel shook his head.

"You need to take a break to make sure you don't miss a thing. Nicholas and I will head out as soon as we have the search warrant, and also check on Adams."

Liam started to argue, but Lorelai jumped into the fray. "Liam, please. Miguel is right and none of us wants to see you fall flat on your face."

"Really? Not even you?" he said, eyes narrowed as he gazed at his ex.

With a roll of her eyes, she said, "Not even me," and hurried from the room.

"I guess I'll go," Liam said and walked away, leaving Miguel, Nicholas, David and Maisy behind.

Miguel glanced at Nicholas. "Can you please follow up on the search warrant?"

"Will do," Nicholas said and headed to his office to check.

"We could use your skills later, David. I know you had a late night so why don't you go get some rest as well and come back in a few hours."

Unlike Liam, David didn't argue. "I'll be back after lunch," he said and left.

Miguel sat beside Maisy and took her hand into his. "You didn't get much rest last night either," he said and loved the bright splash of color that erupted across her cheeks.

"No thanks to you, only…" She paused, uneasy, and peered around the room. Seemingly satisfied that anything they said would be private, she said, "Where do we go from here? Back to our old lives?"

"Isn't that what you want? Travel. Adventure."

She barked out a rough laugh and shook her head.

"I think I've had my share of adventure for a little while. Home is looking good and with the Crusader in custody, there are lots of places in Seattle that I can feature on my blog."

"And maybe you could even share your experience with the Crusader and the FBI, private parts omitted of course," he said and chuckled.

HE HAD A wry smile on his face and Maisy wasn't quite sure what to make of his slightly less serious demeanor this morning. Especially about a subject as serious as what the future would hold for them. But she didn't want to weigh down the discussion quite so soon.

"I don't know, Miguel. I bet some people would be interested in how the FBI works undercovers," she teased and got a kick out of how a stain of color worked across his cheeks.

"I think the only person I want interested is you, Maisy. It's not what I expected when this investigation started, believe me," he admitted with a wag of his head.

"Me either, but here we are, and I can't imagine not having you in my life, as hard as it might be," she said and cupped his cheek.

"It is hard. Dangerous. And I can't ask you to live with that fear. With the possibility that one day—"

She didn't let him finish, laying her thumb across his lips to silence him. "I know you've seen that first-hand with your mom."

"And with her partner, who was killed with her. He left behind his wife and a newborn. I saw her pain and the loss."

"Pain and loss are part of life sometimes, but do you know what's sadder? Never having loved at all. Never experiencing what we've experienced in the last few days. That comfort and peace. The joy that I found in your arms," she said, leaned forward and kissed him.

THE FEEL OF HER LIPS, the warmth of them, broke through the chill in his heart at the thought of not having her in his life. He answered her kiss, meeting her mouth with his over and over until they were breathless.

Only then did he break apart from her, but he leaned his forehead on hers and skimmed his hand through the caramel locks of her hair. "You are a determined woman. A strong woman."

"A woman who can handle a life like yours," she said, trying to convince him, only that wasn't necessary.

"You can handle anything, I think, including a life with me. It's why I want you in my life. Today. Tomorrow. Forever. That is if you'll have me," he said.

A smile slowly erupted across her features, brightening the blue of her gaze to the color of a summer sky. "If that's a proposal, the answer is yes."

"Then there's only one thing that would make me

happier—how soon can you marry me?" he said and dropped a playful kiss on her lips.

She chuckled and shook her head. "I think I like this new impulsive side of you."

In truth, she made him feel lighter, as if the weight of the world that had descended on him with the deaths of his mom and her partner was no longer holding him down. "It's thanks to you. You've set me free of the past."

She leaned her forehead against his again and said, "Just like you've set me free. Together we can do this."

"We can. If you don't mind, I'd like to go see my dad. Tell him the good news. Let him know that he's free to move around now that we've caught the Crusader."

"I'd like that as well," she said, rose, and held out her hand to him. "I'd like to go now, if you can, that is."

Miguel looked toward Nicholas's office. "Let me just check with Nicholas about the search warrant."

"Sounds good," she said, and he hurried off to his team member, who was on the phone with someone.

As Nicholas hung up, Miguel said, "How are we doing?"

Nicholas leaned back in his chair and laced his hands together behind his head in a casual pose. "They're getting the judge out of bed to sign the warrant. May be another hour before we have it so I may go get a shower and change if that's okay with you."

"It is. Maisy and I are just going to see my dad. We have some good news for him," Miguel said with a smile.

Nicholas's gaze skipped from him to where Maisy waited in their work area. "Let me guess. You and Maisy—"

"I proposed," Miguel jumped in, surprised by his own excitement at the prospect.

Nicholas did a quick wag of his head. "I have to admit, I never thought I'd see this day, but I'm happy for you. I think Maisy will be good for you and that you'll be good for her."

Miguel looked back toward her and smiled. "I think so. Now, if only Liam would see what a mistake he made."

Nicholas nodded. "I think he may have. I overheard him saying something to David just before he left."

"Let's hope so. I'm not sure I can take more of the Lorelai-Liam drama in the office," he said and gestured to Maisy. "We're going to visit with my father, but I'll be back within the hour. Hopefully we'll have the search warrant by then."

"Hopefully. I'll see you later and…I'm happy for you, Miguel."

"And I'm happy for you, Nicholas. When you first met Aubrey during that serial killer investigation, I have to confess I was worried, but I see how happy she's made you," Miguel said.

"I am happy. More than I ever thought possible

so if you'll excuse me, I'm heading home," Nicholas said and shot out of his chair.

"I'll see you later," Miguel said and followed Nicholas out the door to where his team member paused to congratulate Maisy.

She hugged the other agent and after, walked to his side and twined her fingers with his. "Ready to go?"

Ready? he asked himself, but didn't hesitate to say, "More ready than I ever thought."

Chapter Twenty

Liam juggled the flowers as he rode the elevator up to the BAU offices, which he'd left just a little over two hours earlier.

He'd gone home as instructed and as soon as his head hit the pillow, he'd fallen asleep. But the moment he'd opened his eyes, he'd known what he had to do without delay.

The elevator door had barely opened when he rushed out, pushed through the doors of the BAU offices and hurried to the director's anteroom, where Lorelai was seated at her desk.

She looked up as he approached and seemed surprised that he was there. Surprised but pleased, he told himself.

"Good morning, Lorelai," he said and held out the bouquet of flowers to her, but she didn't take them or return the greeting.

Fear gripped his gut, but he pushed on. "I know I've hurt you and I'm sorry. But when I called off the wedding, it wasn't because of you—it was because of me. Because I was afraid that I would mess things up the way my family messed things up."

Lorelai wagged her head and blew out a rough sigh. "You are not your father or your mother, Liam. You don't have to make their mistakes again," she stressed.

"I should have known that, but when I realized you were at the station with the bomber, it hit me. Hard. I didn't want to lose you," he said and held out the flowers to her again, holding his breath that this time she wouldn't refuse them. Refuse him. "Please marry me, Lorelai. This week, like we had originally planned."

"It's not that easy," Lorelai said, but took the flowers from him and smiled. "Carnations. My favorites."

"It is that easy. I called the restaurant. They haven't rebooked our room yet. The minister's still available also. Please forgive me and say yes. Make me a very happy man."

She dipped her head to the bouquet and inhaled the spicy fragrance of the carnations. As she lifted her gaze to meet his, she smiled and said, "Yes."

THE HOTEL ROOM door flew open as soon as Miguel knocked. "Thank God you're both okay. I just saw the news on TV," his father said and invited them into the room. "We're fine, Dad," Miguel said and his father narrowed his gaze as they walked into the room hand-in-hand.

"I'm so glad, Miguel. You know how I worry

about you," his father said and followed them into the room.

Miguel shared a quick glance with Maisy, but then smiled. "I know you worry, but I think you'll be happy to hear that Maisy agreed to marry me."

Robert smiled and his gaze sheened with tears. He walked over and hugged Maisy and then Miguel. "I am so happy. I think I worried as much, maybe more, about you being so alone."

Maisy hugged Robert and said, "Well, you don't have to worry about that anymore. I think Miguel and I will be very happy together."

His father's teary gaze skipped from Maisy to him. "I know you will be. You've made this old man very happy."

"And we're very happy, Dad. I hope that you'll think about spending more time in Seattle," Miguel said.

This time the tears, of joy and not sorrow, slipped down his father's cheeks. "I think I will. Maybe even move here, that is if you don't think I'll be intruding."

Maisy laid a hand on his jacket sleeve and smiled. "I know this is all so sudden, but I think it would be wonderful to have you here."

"I agree, Dad. You can even help us plan the wedding," Miguel said.

"A wedding. You and Maisy! How wonderful," he said and hugged them once again.

It is wonderful, Miguel thought and savored the

peace of the embrace with his father and Maisy. It was a peace he'd never expected, but he welcomed it.

In their arms, he was finally free of the pain of the past. Free to forge a future and a family with this amazing woman.

MIGUEL HUGGED MAISY to him as they moved to the languid beats of the slow dance. He brushed a kiss across her temple and said, "This is nice."

She skimmed a kiss along his jaw and said, "It is. Everyone seems so happy."

Miguel looked around at his team members as they danced with their significant others. Madeline and Jackson. Dashiell and Raina. Nicholas and Aubrey. Liam and Lorelai, dressed in their wedding best.

They all looked so happy and he hoped they were as happy as Maisy and him.

Caitlyn Yang stood off to one side of the room with her boyfriend, David beside them with his girlfriend.

My team, he thought with pride at what they'd been able to accomplish in the past few months. Catching a serial killer. Freeing a young child from a kidnapper. Proving Dashiell's sister was not an embezzler. Stopping Richard Rothwell and his rampage as the Seattle Crusader.

It had taken them the past week to tie up all the loose ends. Adams, who had planted the bombs, had luckily survived his wounds and together with Davis, the licensed blaster, had provided them the last bits of evidence needed to create an airtight case against Rothwell. If there was one thing that bothered him it was that the U.S. attorney had agreed to accept Rothwell's guilty plea in exchange for a reduced sentence. Miguel had thought Rothwell should serve the maximum sentence considering all the harm he'd done in order to win the state senate seat and make some cash from the insurance payouts on the bombed buildings he owned. Still, thirty years in jail might be the equivalent of a life sentence given Rothwell's age.

And I've been freed from my life sentence of loneliness by meeting Maisy, he thought and bent his head to kiss her.

She kissed him back and he could feel her smile against his lips. It dragged a smile to his lips as they kissed again and again.

But then a sound and vibration crept into his awareness, pulling him away from the joyful moment.

He yanked his smartphone from his jacket pocket. *Director Branson.*

"Good evening, Olivia," he said and as his team members heard her name, they looked his way and stopped dancing.

"Good evening, Miguel. I'm so, so sorry to interrupt your celebration and please wish Liam and Lorelai my best," she said, her tone contrite.

"I will and I know you wouldn't be calling unless it was important," he said and little by little his team members drifted over to hear the discussion.

"It is. We have a new case and I'm sending all the information to you. I need the team to review it and be ready to discuss it in an hour," she said.

Miguel glanced at his team members' faces and had no doubt. They were the FBI Seattle BAU team and could tackle any case that came their way.

"We'll be ready."

* * * * *

Don't miss the previous books in the Behavioral Analysis Unit series:

Profiling a Killer *by Nichole Severn*
Decoding a Criminal *by Barb Han*
Tracing a Kidnapper *by Juno Rushdan*

*Available now
wherever Harlequin Intrigue books are sold!*

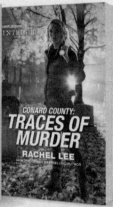

COMING NEXT MONTH FROM

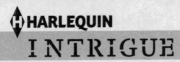

#2031 TEXAS STALKER
An O'Connor Family Mystery • by Barb Han

While fleeing an attempt on her life, Brianna Adair is reunited with her childhood friend Garrett O'Connor. Trusting others is not in her nature, but Brianna will have to lean on the gorgeous rancher or risk falling prey to a stalker who won't stop until she's dead...

#2032 STAY HIDDEN
Heartland Heroes • by Julie Anne Lindsey

Running from her abuser is Gina Ricci's only goal, and disappearing completely may be the answer. But local private investigator Cruz Winchester wants to arrest her ex and set Gina free. When everyone in Gina's life seems to become a target, will Cruz be able to save them all...without sacrificing Gina or her unborn child?

#2033 ROGUE CHRISTMAS OPERATION
Fugitive Heroes: Topaz Unit • by Juno Rushdan

Resolved to learn the truth of her sister's death, Hope Fischer travels to the mysterious military-controlled town where her sister worked at Christmas. Teaming up with the enigmatic Gage Graham could lead to the answers she's looking for—if Gage's secret past doesn't find and kill them first.

#2034 K-9 PATROL
Kansas City Crime Lab • by Julie Miller

After his best friend's sister, KCPD criminalist Lexi Callahan, is attacked at a crime scene, K-9 officer Aiden Murphy and partner Blue will do anything to protect her. But being assigned as her protection detail means spending every minute together. Can Aiden overcome his long-buried feelings for Lexi in time to save her from a killer?

#2035 FIND ME
by Cassie Miles

Searching for her childhood best friend requires undercover FBI agent Isabel "Angie" D'Angelo to infiltrate the Denver-based Lorenzo crime family. Standing in her way is Julian Parisi, a gentleman's club manager working for the Lorenzo family. Angie will need to convince Julian to help even though she knows he's got secrets of his own...

#2036 DEADLY DAYS OF CHRISTMAS
by Carla Cassidy

Still recovering from a previous heartbreak, Sheriff Mac McKnight avoids Christmas at any cost, even with his deputy, Callie Stevens, who loves the holidays—and him. But when a serial killer's victims start mirroring *The Twelve Days of Christmas*, he'll have to confront his past...and his desire for Callie.

YOU CAN FIND MORE INFORMATION ON UPCOMING HARLEQUIN TITLES, FREE EXCERPTS AND MORE AT HARLEQUIN.COM.

HICNM1021

"So, tell me who you *think* is stalking you," he said in more of a statement than a question.

She shrugged her shoulders. "I don't know. That's a tough one. There's a guy in one of my classes who creeps me out. I'll be taking notes furiously in class only to get a weird feeling like I'm being watched and then look up to see him staring at me intensely."

"Has he come around the bar?"

"A time or two," she admitted.

"Is he alone?"

"As far as I can tell. He never has worked up the courage to come talk to me, so he takes a table by the dance floor and nurses a beer," she said.

"Any idea what his name is?"

"Derk Waters, I think. I overheard someone say that in a group project when his team was next to mine. By the way, there should be no group projects in college. I end up doing all the work and have to hear complaints from everyone in the process," she said as an aside.

Garrett chuckled. "Maybe you should learn to let others pull their own weight."

She blew out a sharp breath. "And risk a failing grade? No, thanks. Besides, I tried that once and ended up staying up all night to redo someone's work because they slapped their part together."

HIEXP1021

"Sounds like something you'd do," Garrett said.

"What's that supposed to mean?" She heard the defensiveness in her own voice, but it was too late to reel it in.

"You always were the take-charge type. I'm not surprised you'd pull out a win in a terrible situation."

Well, she really had overreacted. She exhaled, trying to release some of the tension she'd been holding in her shoulders. "Thanks for the compliment, Garrett. It means a lot coming from you. I mean, your opinion matters to me."

"No problem." He shrugged off her comment, but she could see that it meant something to him, too. He picked up his coffee cup and took another sip. "Okay, so we have one creep on the list. What about others?"

"I wouldn't classify this guy as a creep necessarily, but he has followed me out to the parking lot at school more than once. He's a TA, so basically a grad student working for one of my professors. He made it a known that he'd be willing to help if I fell behind in class," she said.

Again, that jaw muscle clenched.

"Doesn't he take a hint?"

"Honestly, he's harmless. The only reason I brought him up was because we were talking about school and for some reason he popped into my mind. He's working his way through school and I doubt he'd risk his future if he got caught," she surmised. "Plus, this person is trying to run me off the road."

"You rejected him. That could anger a certain personality type," he said. "What's his name?"

"Blaine something. I don't remember his last name." Up to this point, she hadn't really believed the slimeball could be someone she knew. A cold shiver raced down her spine at the thought. "I've been working under the assumption one of the guys at the bar meant to get a little too friendly."

"We have to start somewhere. I believe my brothers would say the most likely culprit is someone you know. I've heard them say a woman's biggest physical threat is from those closest to her. Boyfriend. Spouse. Someone in her circle." He shot a look of apology. "It's an awful truth."

She issued a sharp sigh. "I can't even imagine who would want to hurt me."

Don't miss
Texas Stalker *by Barb Han,*
available November 2021 wherever
Harlequin Intrigue books and ebooks are sold.

Harlequin.com